Mel Bay presents

HARMONIC MECHANISMS FOR GUITAR

By George Van Eps

I wish to dedicate these books with love and respect to my late wife Josephine Inglima Van Eps —

George Van Eps

ACKNOWLEDGEMENT

I wish to express my appreciation and gratitude to my daughter Kay Van Eps Adikes for her invaluable assistance in the long process of preparing this series of books —

1 2 3 4 5 6 7 8 9 0

MEL BAY

I0808767

FOREWORD

This volume completes the series of three books concerning harmonic mechanisms.

The term "mechanisms" is used, because the mechanisms are both physical and mental.

In using the word "complete" I am not inferring that these books cover all the many facets of harmony or guitar playing—they pertain to just the areas that have held the greatest interest for me over the years.

A Late Acknowledgement To An Early Friend

When I was in my early teens, I had the good fortune to get to know Ralph Wylie, Professor Ralph Wylie.

Professor Wylie was a master musicologist, philosopher, teacher, etc. and luckily for us, a friend of the Van Eps family.

My brothers; Fred, Robert, and John, studied with him. I didn't, I regret to say, but there was a lot of "rub off."

Prof, as he was known to his intimate friends, did not tell one "how" to do it, he would tell his students "how not" to do it—Prof always encouraged individuality and his choice of words was always flawless, his observations and comments never failed to be very interesting and wise.

Prof was a very soft spoken man, one had to strain to hear what he was saying, and his wordage was almost always indirectly straight to the point.

If Prof were alive today he probably would say something like this about my work: "If you will give the subject your undivided attention one more time, it will undoubtedly be that much better."

All who have known Professor Ralph Wylie miss his very colorful, articulate, artistic personality.

GENERAL REMARKS

A teacher must not impose or force musical preferences or styles on the student —

A conscientious teacher must strive to fan the students spark of individuality and inventiveness into a raging fire.

An instrument in good condition is not unlike a computer in this sense; the output cannot be any better than the input —

The closest, most intimate relationship we will every enjoy is the relationship between ourselves and our instrument, because this is when the two entities must become one —

I have been told, and of course, I realize that my grammar at times is a bit unusual, but after all, the subject is not grammar.

I'm also known to be quite redundant at times—most of the time as a matter of fact, but, I've found over the years, "things" must be pictured and explained many different ways in the hope that one of them will find an open door into the mind.

There are certain aspects of each concept that are related and linked together, as will be noted when studied, but, the basic principles of each are different and individual.

Become familiar with the subtle differences in them.

GENERAL REMARKS
THE LEFT HAND—
A PRECISION MEASURING DEVICE

The left hand must become capable of judging distances and attitudes very accurately.

The fingers, after the hand has delivered them to where they are to function, must be able to judge distances in all directions simultaneously. They must judge long, awkward spreads of all kinds down to distances of just a few thousandths of an inch, example:

The average business card is about seven thousandths of an inch thick. When an inner voice is moving on the 2nd, 3rd, 4th, 5th, strings while the adjoining strings are sounding, the fingers only have half the thickness of that card to play with. In other words, an error of three and one half thousandths of an inch will stifle the notes on the adjoining strings.

Always remember that vibrating strings make the space for fingers much much smaller.

Well trained hands do not have to rely on the eyes to guide them —

A RUDIMENTAL DESCRIPTION OF THE CONCEPTS IN THIS VOLUME:

The Stagger Concept

The "C" has been staggered up one scale step, the result is then frozen and taken through the scales —

The Satellite Concept

This is satellite note motion; every note in the chromatic scale has two satellite notes, one a half tone above, the other a half tone below, they move any direction one half tone at a time —

The Displaced Concept

This triad has been displaced twice into other keys — first from "C" to "E" flat, then to "G" flat etc.

The Progressive Motion Concept

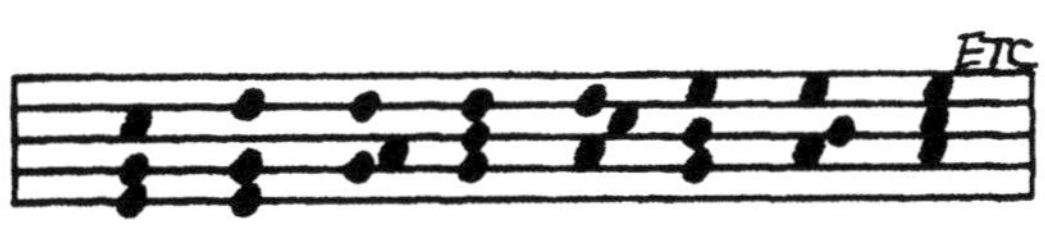

All the notes of any chord moved one at a time thru all notes of the "Grande" arpeggios

GENERAL REMARKS
CHEMISTRY

The fingering and string set markings in many of the studies in these books are varied, and may at times skip around the fingerboard purposely, because, the intent is to present as many different fingering combinations as space will permit.

There are many more than shown, of course; and one must endeavor to find as many as possible.

Fingerboard chemistry is not only tonal, for mechanical chemistry is also involved.

A chain of combined mechanisms to produce notes, is necessary, to complete any harmonic scale, phrase, passage, progression, etc.

A blending of all these different chemistrys results in: "combined tones," plus "mixed mechanics," of which the sum total is: "music."

Except for special articulation, very little right hand fingering is indicated for the following reasons: The majority of people interested in studying these books are already familiar with the various right hand styles, and will govern themselves accordingly.

There are many ways of sounding the strings—the most common are:
the plecturm (pick)—alternation is best for velocity—(up and down strokes)
the fingers (classic)—again, alternation is best for velocity—(taking turns)
the fingers and pick combined—usually a mixture, with both alternating —

The classic finger style offers the greatest advantage because of being able to utilize all five fingers.

The material presented in this series of books is most suited to the classic right hand and the combination of fingers and plectrum.

These studies are meant to be tools to build musical structures. How to use them must be dictated by one's ear and taste, sense of proportion and balance. The ear knows pleasing sounds, and the combinations of sound.
It must never be said that "this" is the only way to do it. However, I do feel that with careful study these books can provide many of the ways to play difficult, complicated harmonics.

STRING CHART

EXPLANATION OF THE STRING SET SYMBOLS:

A vertical or angled line thus– / –means "Set"—
The number in front of it is the set number—
The number after it indicates the number of strings employed—
Example:
When the 1st-2nd-3rd-strings are employed the symbol is:
1/3—The first set of three–etc.
When the 1st-2nd-3rd-4th-strings are employed the symbol is:
1/4—The 1st set of four–etc.

THE BROKEN AND THE DIVIDED SETS:

Example:
When the 1st-2nd-4th-strings are employed (skipping the 3rd string) it is termed a broken set—the symbol is:
1/B3—The first set of broken three–etc.
When the order is reversed, (skipping the 2nd instead of the 3rd string) the word "broken" is used first, thus:
B1/3—The broken first set of three–etc.

When the 1st-2nd-4th-5th-strings are employed it is termed a divided set—the symbol is:
D1/4—The divided first set of four–etc.
When the 1st-3rd-5th-strings are employed the symbol is:
1/D3—The first set of divided three—and so on—
When the 1st-4th-strings are employed the symbol is:
A 1—
When the 2nd-5th-strings are employed the symbol is:
A 2—etc.
When the 1st-5th-strings are employed the symbol is:
B 1—etc.

NOTE
A symbol for the 1st-3rd-4th-6th-strings is not necessary because it would encompass all of the strings, therefore, the very notation dictates where and on what strings the notes are located.

STRING SET CHART

SYMBOLS:—STRINGS EMPLOYED—

1/2—1st-2nd-
2/2—2nd-3rd-
3/2—3rd-4th-
4/2—4th-5th-
5/2—5th-6th-

1/3—1st-2nd-3rd-
2/3—2nd-3rd-4th-
3/3—3rd-4th-5th-
4/3—4th-5th-6th-

1/4—1st-2nd-3rd-4th-
2/4—2nd-3rd-4th-5th-
3/4—3rd-4th-5th-6th-

1/5—1st-2nd-3rd-4th-5th-
2/5—2nd-3rd-4th-5th-6th-

THE BROKEN AND DIVIDED SETS:

1/B2—1st-3rd-
2/B2—2nd-4th-
3/B2—3rd-5th-
4/B2—4th-6th-

1/B3—1st-2nd-4th-
2/B3—2nd-3rd-5th-
3/B3—3rd-4th-6th-

B1/3—1st-3rd-4th-
B2/3—2nd-4th-5th-
B3/3—3rd-5th-6th-

1/B4—1st-2nd-3rd-5th-
2/B4—2nd-3rd-4th-6th-

B1/4—1st-3rd-4th-5th-
B2/4—2nd-4th-5th-6th-
1D/3—1st-2nd-5th-
2D/3—2nd-3rd-6th-

1/D3—1st-3rd-5th-
2/D3—2nd-4th-6th-

D1/3—1st-4th-5th-
D2/3—2nd-5th-6th-

D1/4—1st-2nd-4th-5th-
D2/4—2nd-3rd-5th-6th-

A1—1st-4th-
A2—2nd-5th-
A3—3rd-6th-

B1—1st-5th-
B2—2nd-6th-

01—1st-6th-

CHROMATIC CONCEPT REFERENCE PAGE- ODD NUMBERED BARS ARE REGULAR DIATONIC SCALE-EVEN NUMBERED BARS PROVIDE THE CHROMATIC "LINKS"- ALWAYS CHECK WHEN IN DOUBT ABOUT ACCIDENTALS- C MAJOR
-ASCENDING LINKS IN THE KEY OF "B"-DESCENDING LINKS IN "Db"- ASCENSION= BARS 1-2-3-4 ETC.-DESCENSION= BARS 15-14-13-12 ETC.

CHROMATIC CONCEPT REFERENCE PAGE—
ASCENDING LINKS IN "B" MINOR-DESCENDING LINKS IN "Db" MINOR—

"C" HARMONIC MINOR

FOREWORD
GENERAL REMARKS

Most of these studies are based on utilizing the natural tones of the major and minor scales.

All scales are important, very important, particularly the diatonic scales, because the spacing of the tones describe the harmonic/melodic mode of the keys—the mood of the music.

The scales are very comforting, assuring; everything around us changes constantly, the scales do not change—only the use of them changes. And of course at the head of the list of important scales is the chromatic scale from which all scales are born. The chromatic scale is the mother of all scales.

Many people believe the scales to be just a painful formality that must be endured for a short time.

It disturbs me whenever I hear budding young students complain about the nuisance of having to "bother" with scales, because little do they realize that all music whether it be jazz, classical, or any idiom in between demands complete working knowledge of them. It is absolutely essential that scales become firmly embedded in the mind, and physically playable.

CHAPTER 1
ARTICULATED TENTHS

ARTICULATED TENTHS
GENERAL REMARKS

This chapter concerns the open third interval which is the tenth. It is one of the mainstays of harmony, a virtual backbone. It's an interesting, satisfying interval.

When the two notes are sounded together, the result is a solid, meaty, rich duet of tones.

The tenth intervals are almost always present in three and four note open voicings.
Here are just a few very basic examples showing how tenths become the very backbone of "old friend" common guitar chords:

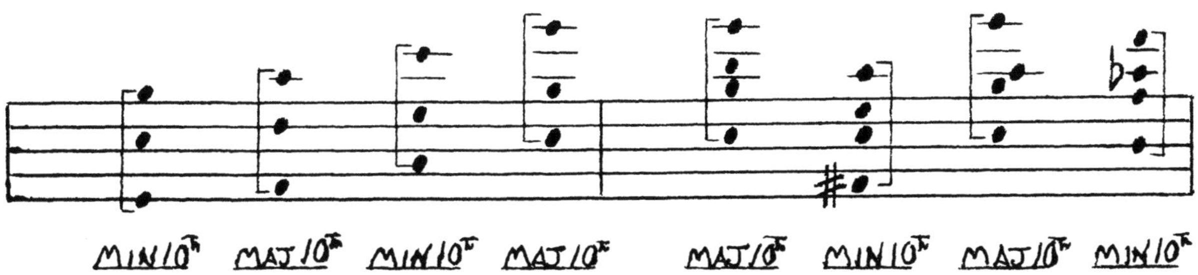

When the upper note of a minor tenth is lowered a half tone, it becomes a ninth interval —
When the upper note of a major tenth is raised a half tone, it becomes an eleventh interval. Both of these intervals will appear occasionally in the arpeggio studies in tenths later on in this chapter.

A walking action very simular to the shifting of weight and balance from one leg to the other is achieved when the pairs of fingers alternate one hundred percent.

Unfortunately, continuous extended alternation is not possible all of the time, therefore, each of the fingers has to be trained to repeat rapidly and accurately, some times on the same string, some times skipping over many strings in order to bridge the gaps in the walking action.

When one finger is used twice in a row such as: 1-2 1-3 etc. to make up two teams the alternation, or walking action is only fifty percent and therefore the machinelike rocker arm articulation is incomplete. In other words, when a finger has to shift from one team to make up another team, there is no walking action.

If our hands had one more finger, the alternation could be continuous thereby making repetition unnecessary.

These studies show some of the many different ways of employing the teams and combinations of teams.

Combinations of fingers make up the various pairs called teams —
Two teams make a working combination and there are many ways to couple the teams —
There are many ways to couple the combinations.

ARTICULATED TENTHS
THE RIGHT HAND ALTERNATION

The right hand fingers must alternate in teams and learn to synchronize precisely with the left hand alternating teams of fingers. The right hand alternating teams are shown in the following examples:

RIGHT HAND REVERSED

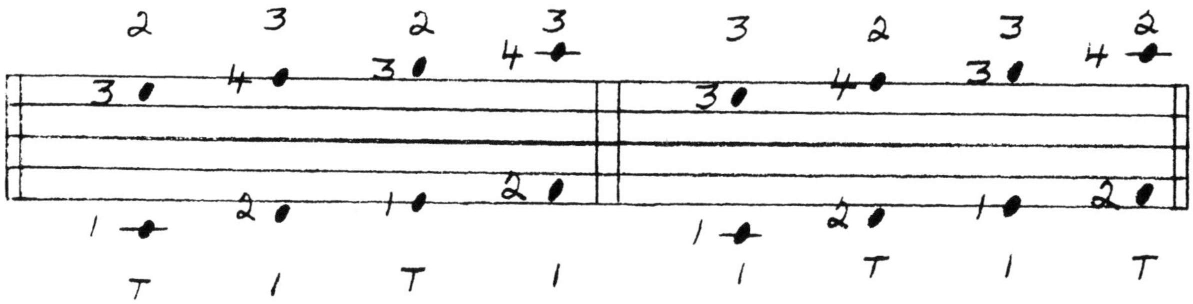

THIS IS VERY GOOD PRACTICE

LEFT HAND REVERSED
RIGHT HAND REVERSED

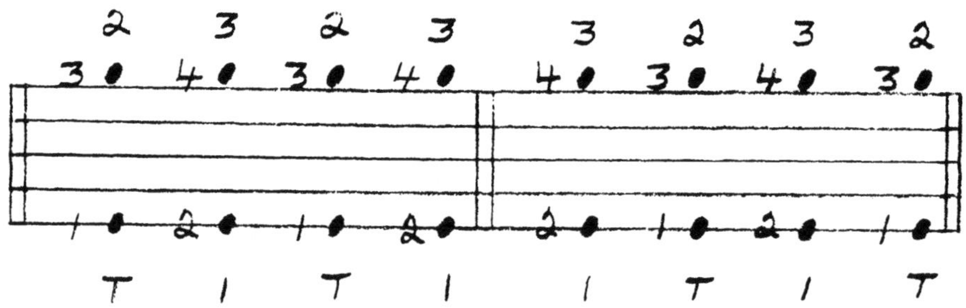

Practice such as this tends to lean away from favoritism — both reversals must be trained to begin a phase. They must be prepared to work.

In these books the thumb is marked with the letter "T", in place of the traditional letter "P".

The way tenths are played accurately and rapidly, is by employing team alternation in both hands. The hands must articulate in perfect unison.

Practice the combined team work very slowly until coordination is achieved.

ARTICULATED TENTHS (WALKING TENTHS)

The finger mechanisms and hand movements employed in these studies are meant to show many varied actual playing conditions.

Some of the combinations are designed to be smooth and flowing — others are designed to train the hand to judge distant register changes rapidly, abruptly.

Some of the combinations are intentionally designed to be awkward and demand very precise hand and finger manipulation — all three are important and necessary in order to be well prepared and become aware of the subtle differences in them.

Under actual playing conditions mixtures of the three are required. The above conditions apply to all team articulation.

Whenever independent alternating teams (pairs) of fingers are taking turns, it becomes absolutely necessary to release the pressure on one pair before sounding the next pair — two tenths must not sound at the same time, unless the effect is desired.

The teams must alternate mechanically similar to the push buttons on a radio — when one is down, the others are up — never two at a time. Pianists finger thirds and other intervals using this principle.

The alternating teams of fingers are: 4 3 _ 3 4 _ 2 4 _ 1 4 _ 1 4
2 1 ‾ 2 1 ‾ 1 3 ‾ 3 2 ‾ 2 3

EXAMPLE:

When played correctly, the notes can be heard very softly without employing the right hand — this is an excellent way to tell whether the fingers are are coming down on the two notes in the tenths simultaneously — all alternate articulation can be checked for preciseness in this manner.

ARTICULATED TENTHS
GENERAL REMARKS

A tie line joining two string set marks, indicates that the crossover from one set to the other lies within the normal reach/span of the hand.

ARTICULATED 10THS - 12 KEYS - ONE OCTAVE - TONIC TO TONIC - MAJOR AND MINOR

ARTICULATED 10THS - MAJOR AND MINOR

CONT.

ARTICULATED TENTHS
GENERAL REMARKS

In certain types of articulation, the first finger is tho't of and used as if it were two independant fingers, because the tip of the finger sounds one note, while the second joint sounds another in this alternating process.

This type of alternation requires the tip of the first finger to just rest on a string (applying no pressure) while the second joint sounds a note — the second joint just rests on the first string when the tip sounds a note. In other words, it is not a typical barre situation, it's more like a rocking motion — a rocking barre.

The example below discribes the placement and motion of the first finger during this action, it shows what the finger has to do step-by-step, while the other fingers are busy doing a normal routine fingering job.

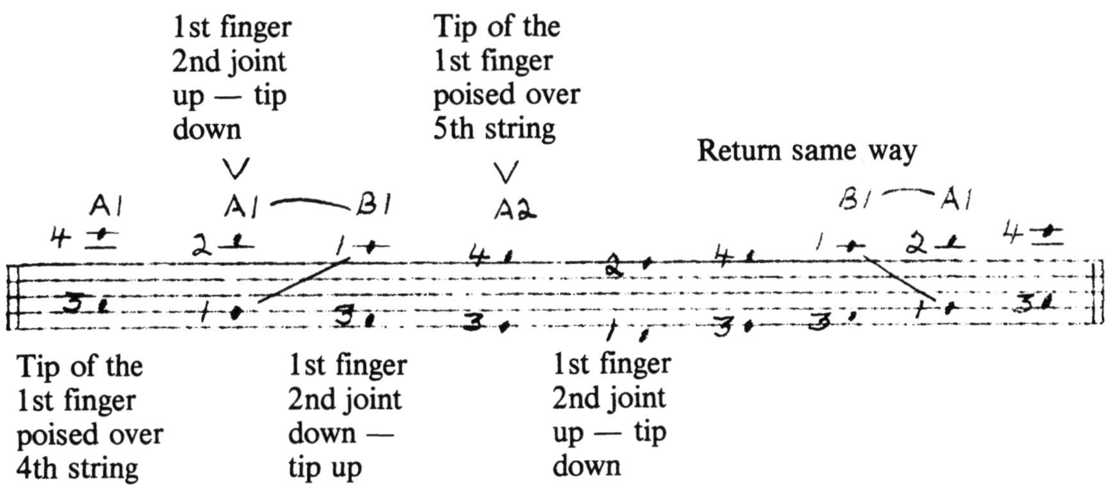

ARTICULATED 10THS - DOUBLE 10THS - 12 KEYS — MAJOR AND MINOR

WHEN STRING SET MARKING CEASES, REPEAT LAST SET OR SETS SHOWN

ARTICULATED 10THS - DOUBLE 10THS

MAJOR AND MINOR

D
DM
G
GM

ARTICULATED 10THS – ARPEGGIO'S – 12 KEYS — MAJOR AND MINOR

DESCEND SAME WAY UNLESS OTHERWISE MARKED

F
F MINOR

Bb
Bb MINOR

Eb
Eb MINOR

Ab
A3
B2 A2
A2
B1 A1
Ab MINOR
A3
B2 A2
A2
B1 A1

D♭
C# MINOR

Gb
F# MINOR– MELODIC MINOR LAST 6 KEYS

B
B MINOR

ARTICULATED 10THS – ARPEGGIO'S

MAJOR AND MINOR

A
A3 A2 A2 A1
A MINOR
A3 A2 A2 A1

ARTICULATED 10THS – ARPEGGIO'S

MAJOR AND MINOR

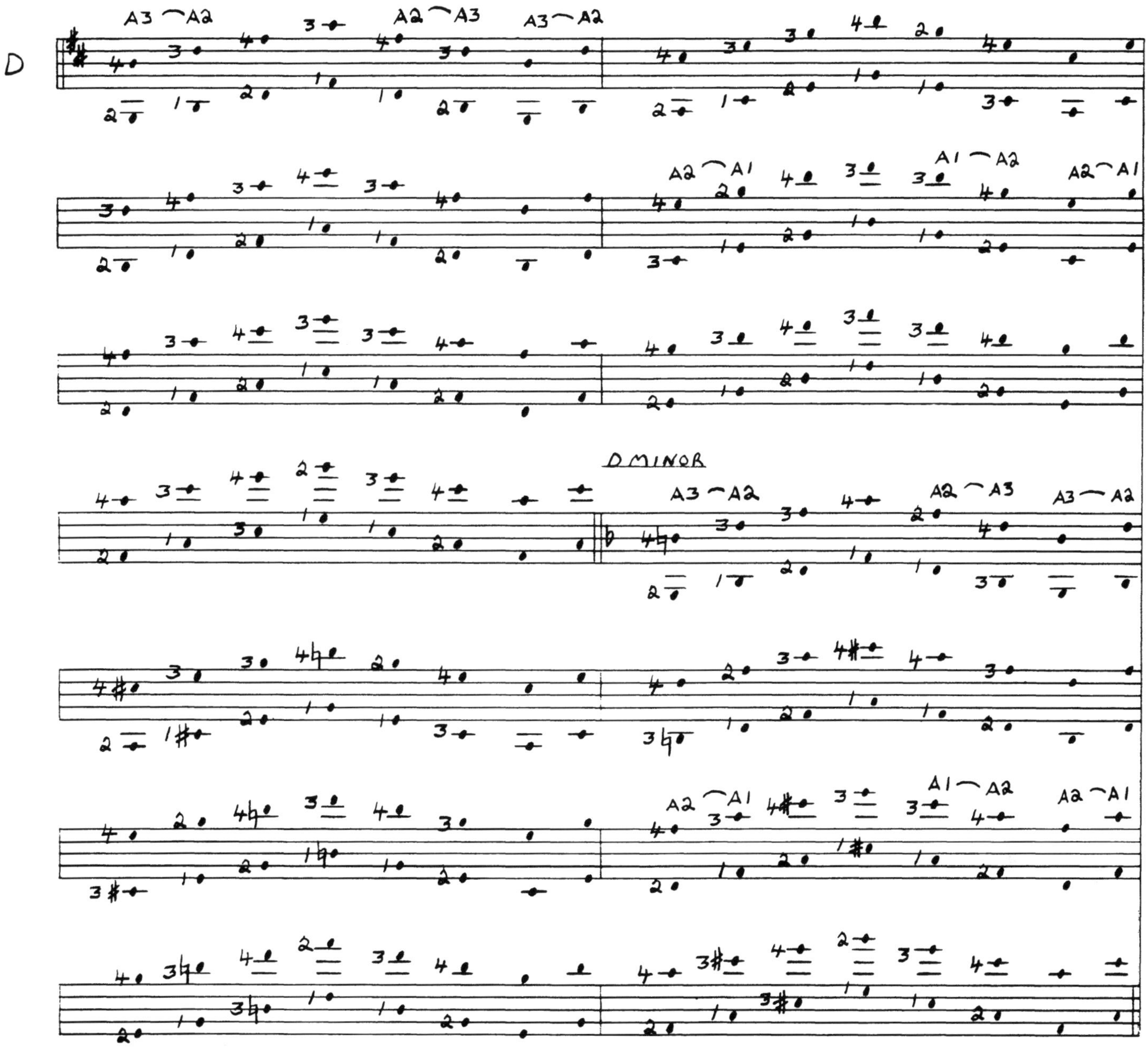

ARTICULATED 10THS ARPEGGIO'S

G

ARTICULATED 10THS – ARPEGGIO'S

MAJOR AND MINOR

C

HARMONIC MINOR 1ST 6 KEYS

CM

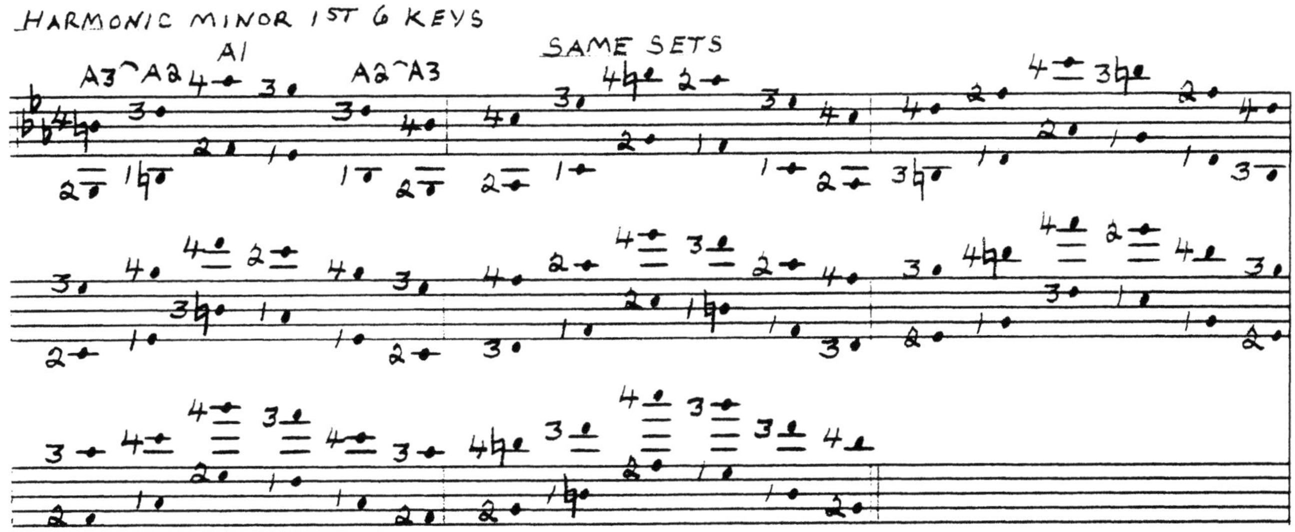

F

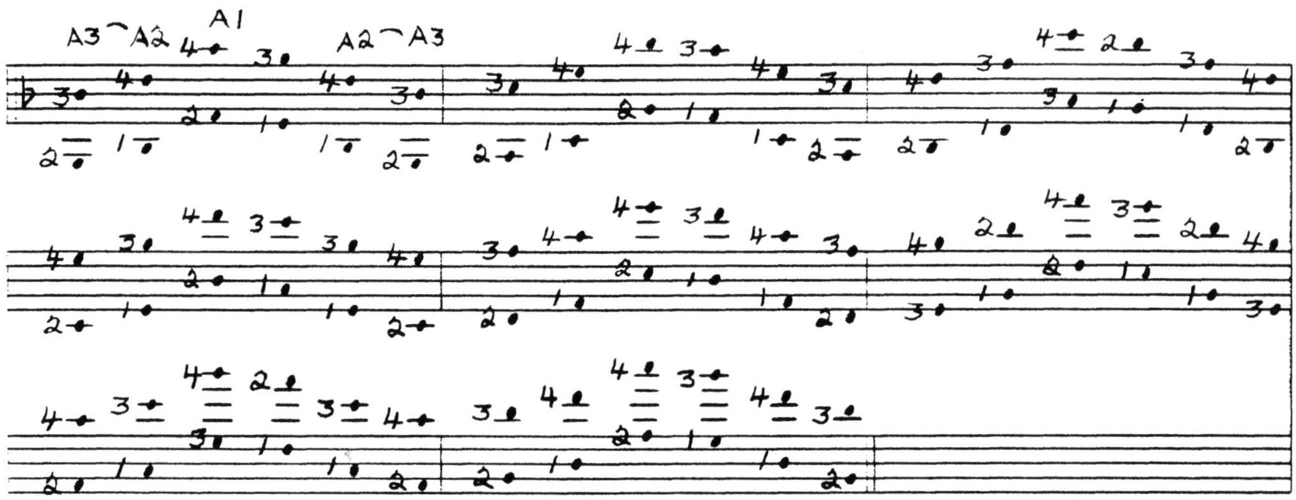

FM

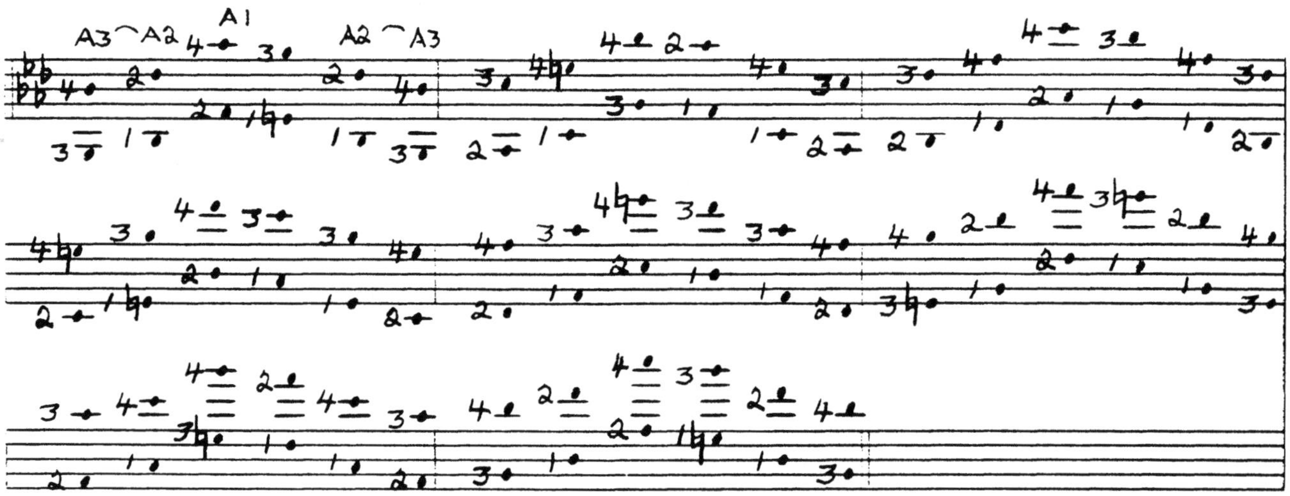

Bb

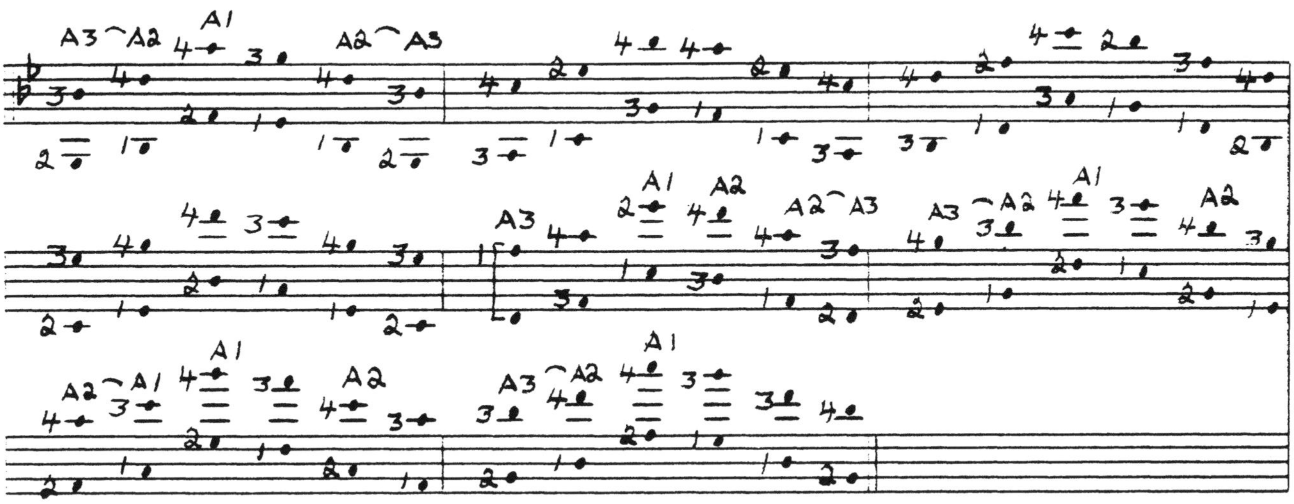

BbM

ARTICULATED 10THS – ARPEGGIO'S MAJOR AND MINOR

Eb

Ebm

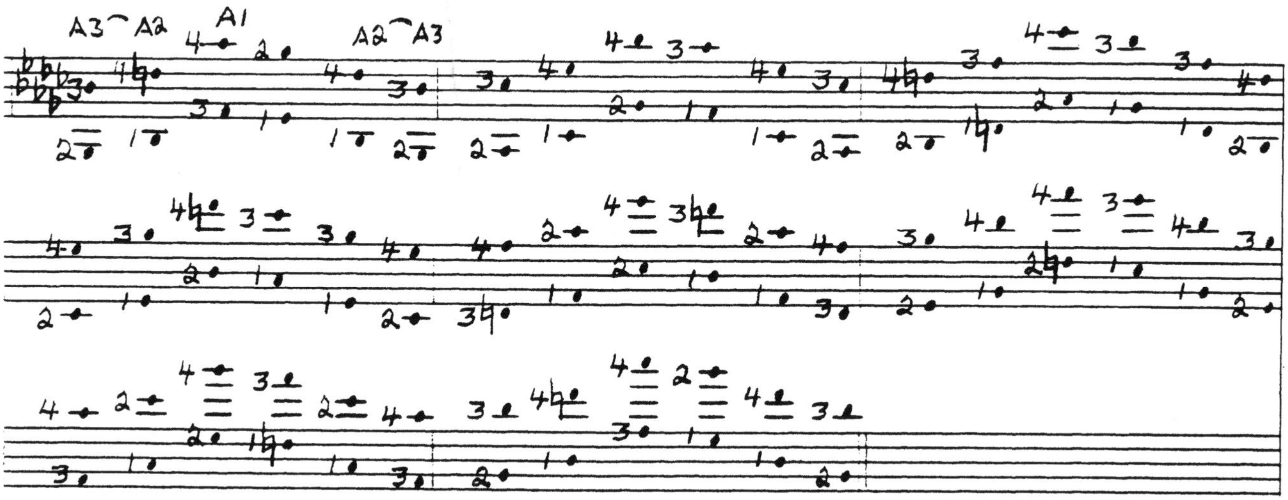

Ab

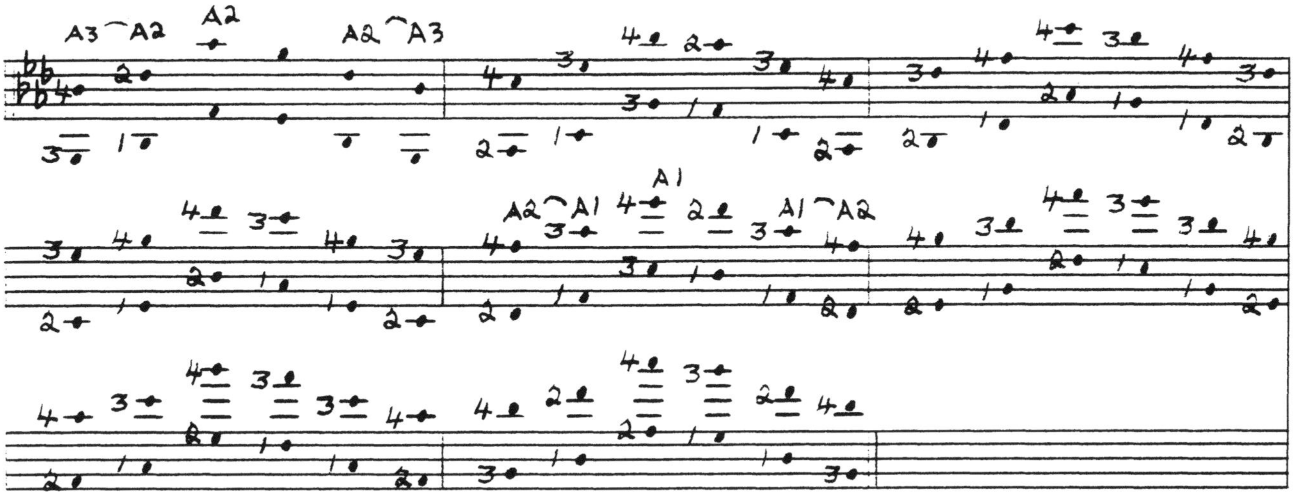

AbM

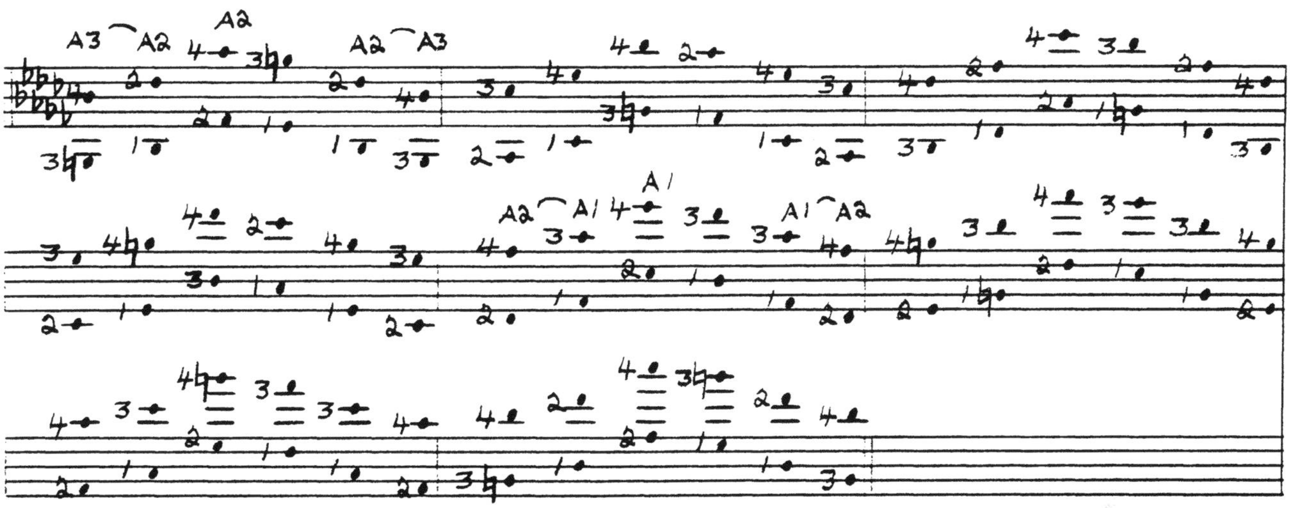

D♭

C♯M

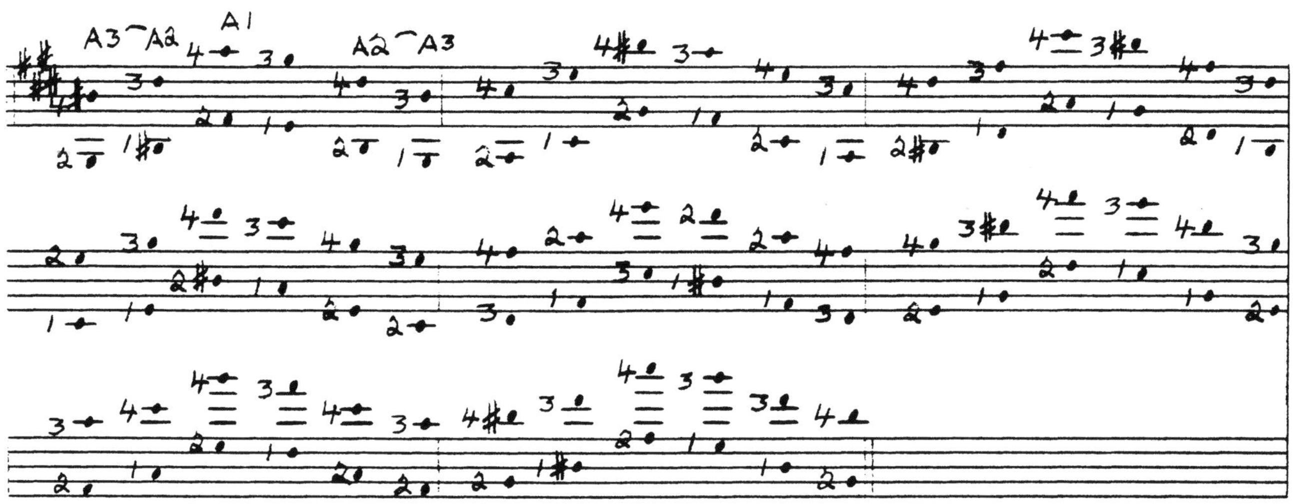

ARTICULATED 10THS – ARPEGGIO'S

MAJOR AND MINOR

MELODIC MINOR LAST 6 KEYS

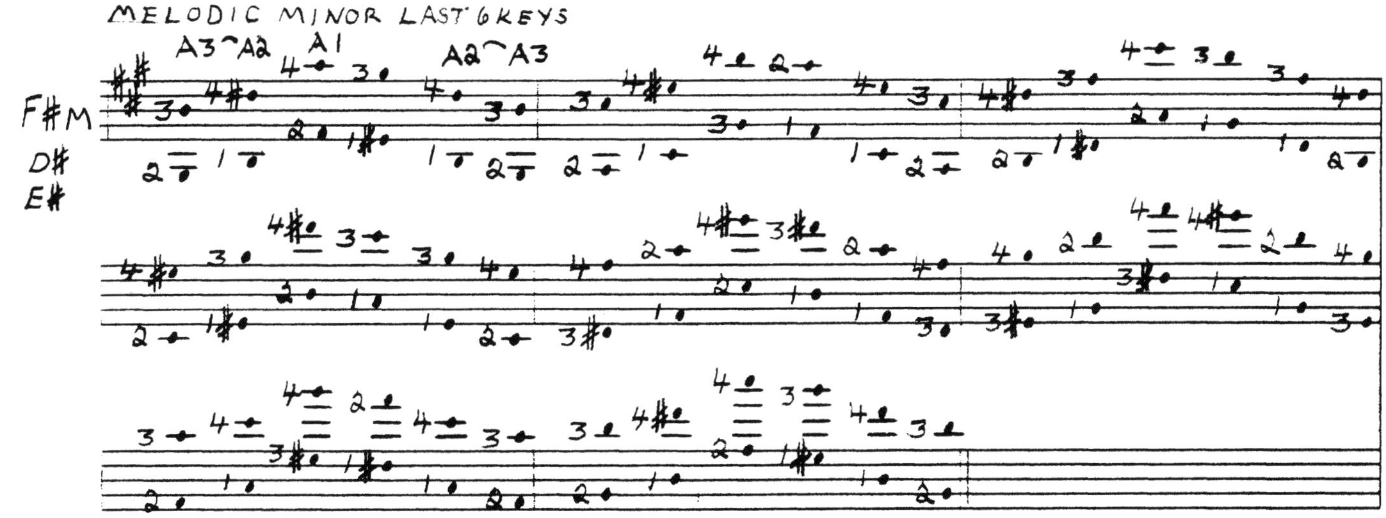

ARTICULATED 10THS – ARPEGGIO'S

MAJOR AND MINOR

B

BM
G#
A#

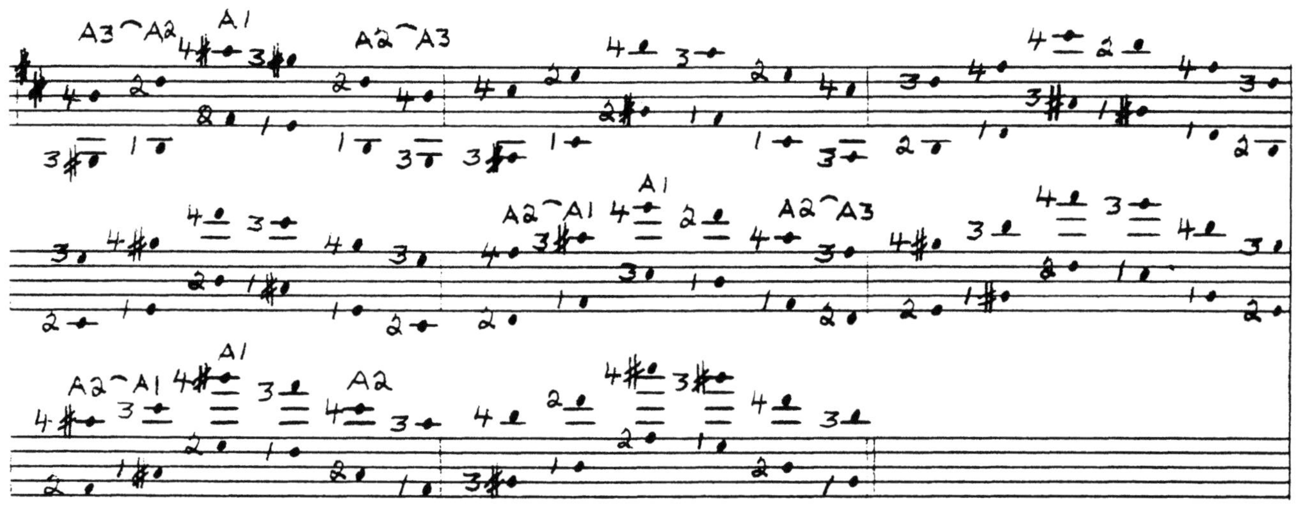

E

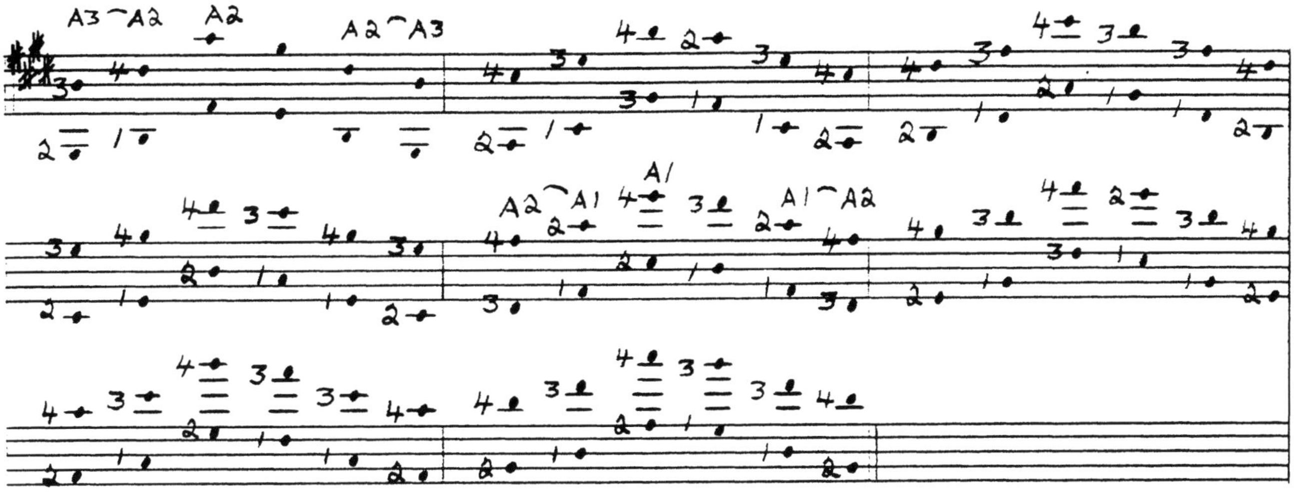

EM
C#
D#

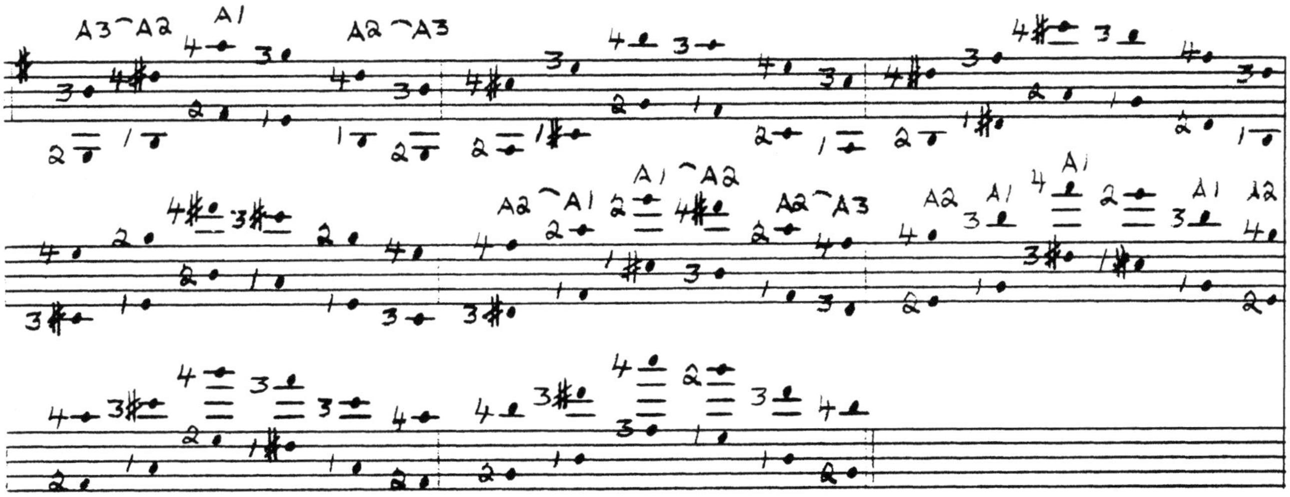

ARTICULATED 10THS – ARPEGGIO'S MAJOR AND MINOR

A

AM
F#
G#

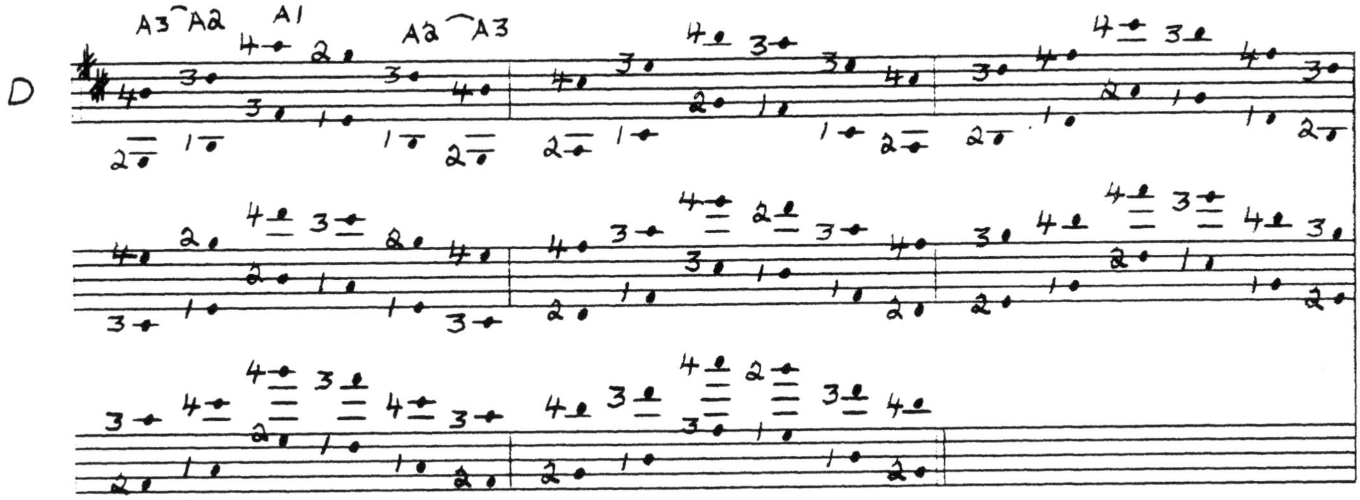
D

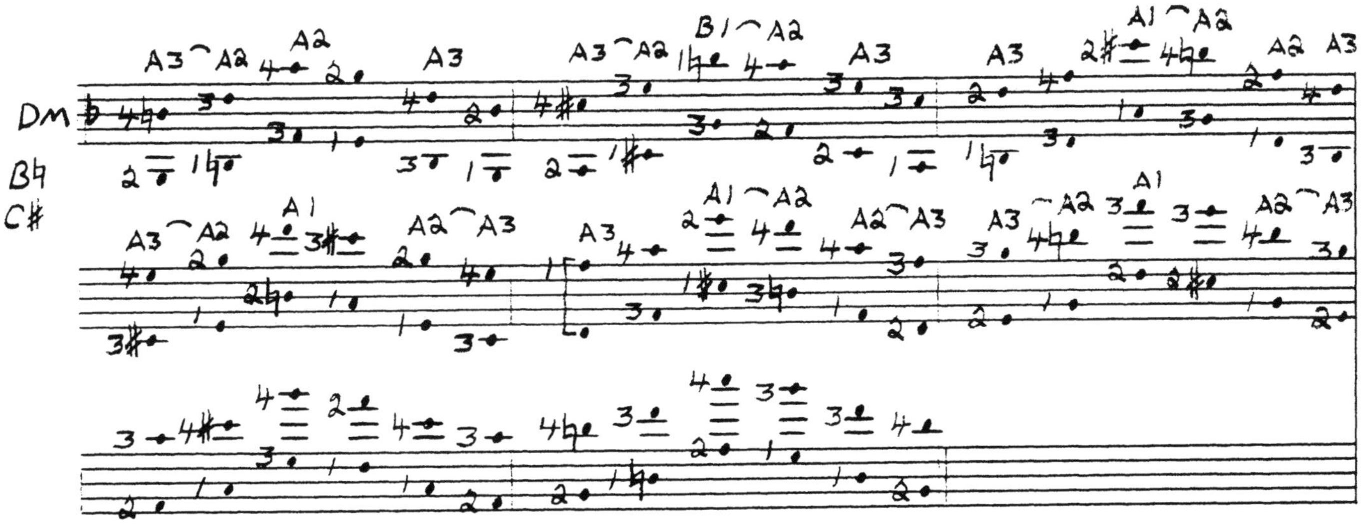
DM
B♮
C♯

ARTICULATED 10THS – ARPEGGIO'S

MAJOR AND MINOR

G

GM
E♮
F#

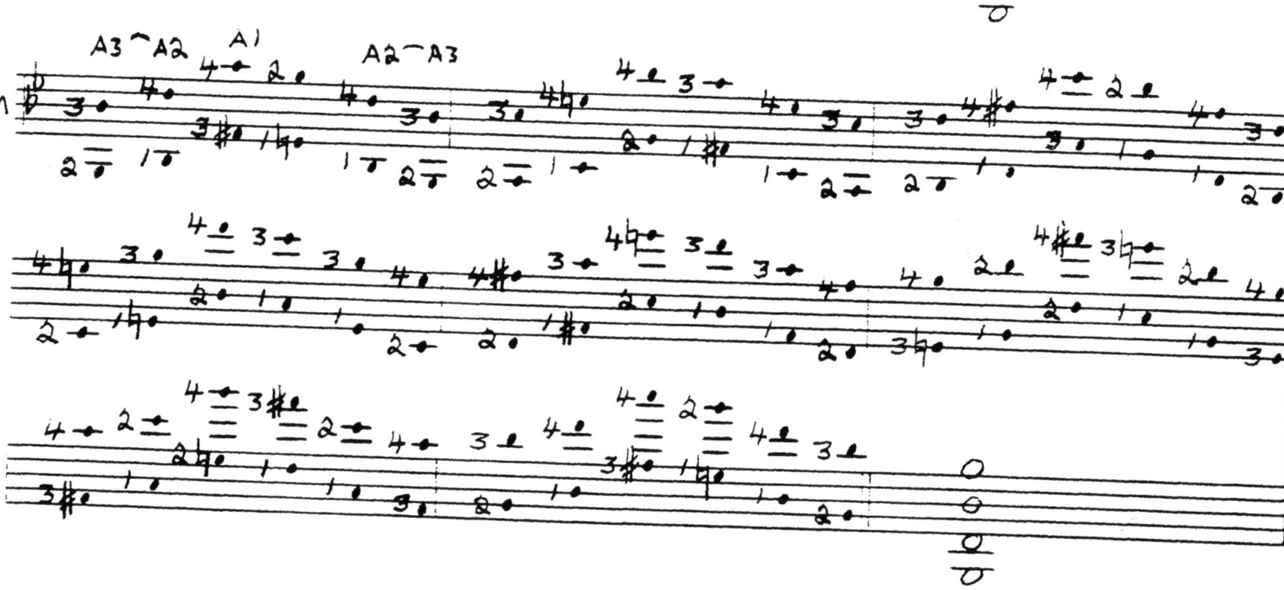

ARTICULATED 10THS ARPEGGIO'S

VARIATIONS - PRACTICE IN MAJOR AND MINOR - ALL KEYS

ALWAYS REVERSE NOTATIONAL PATTERNS - MIX SETS AND FINGERINGS

ARTICULATED TENTHS

Explanation of some of the finger teams employed in these studies.

When tenths merely move one or two steps, the fingering choices are many and simple. The finger teams are different when the tenths continue to move on up or down. The mechanics required to be able to extend the tenths further becomes more exacting. Choosing the right teams of fingers, at the right time is of utmost importance — EXAMPLE:

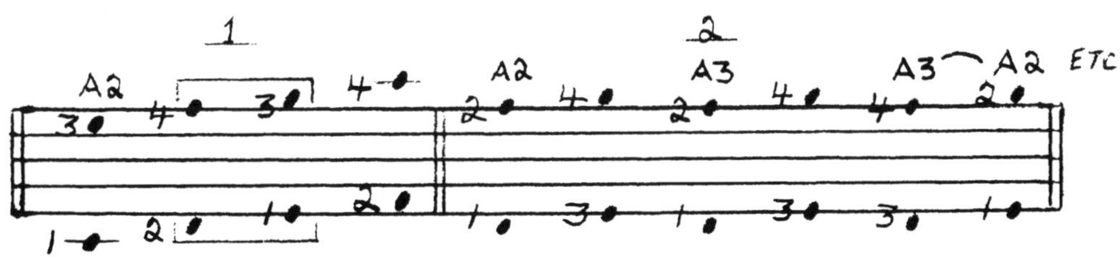

When playing just the bracketed tenths shown in example "one," the finger teams in example "two" are more fluent and practical.
When the tenths continue on up or down as in example "one," the bracketed fingering is necessary in order to be able to continue the walking action this type of articulation describes.
Walking on the fingers as much as possible is absolutely necessary for clean, precise velocity.

ARTICULATED 10THS VARIATIONS

THESE FINGERING SUBTLETIES APPLY MENTALLY AND PHYSICALLY TO ALL MECHANISMS

ARTICULATED 10THS VARIATION EXAMPLES – PLACE MAJOR EXAMPLES IN MINOR – MINOR IN MAJOR EXTEND THEM FULL RANGE – MIX THEM ETC.

ARTICULATED 10THS VARIATIONS

ARTICULATED 10THS VARIATIONS

ARTICULATED TENTHS — VARIATIONS FOLLOWING THE CYCLE OF FIFTHS

In the following study, bar number 2 is in the dominant mode of the key of "F".

It is the second station of the "F" scale, therefore, being on the dominant side of the key of "F" it becomes the "C" step in the circle of keys.

This relationship is present in each two bar pattern throughout the cycle. Take the two bar patterns completely through the circle of keys, one at a time, for overall familiarity and better understanding of the harmonic relationships of the tenths.

ARTICULATED 10THS– VARIATIONS THROUGH THE CIRCLE OF FIFTHS

ARTICULATED 10THS ARPEGGIO'S- EXAMPLES BELOW EXPLAIN THE 9TH AND 11TH INTERVALS

CHAPTER 2
ARTICULATED SIXTHS

ARTICULATED SIXTHS
WALKING SIXTHS

Extend the range of these scale studies up as far as possible and down to the point where the next move would require employing open strings. When the fingerings become familiar, mix them, blend them, make as many different combinations as possible but always begin in a very slow tempo. This is very important because slowing down in the difficult places can become a very bad habit. Tempos should be gauged by, and geared to, the difficult fingering combinations.

When the fingers are not involved with double stops and small barres, they must be in arched (hammer) position.

As has been stated before, working with the "very" difficult makes the difficult much easier, and so on down the line —

It is unwise to put off, or avoid working on awkward, seemingly illogical teams of fingers and combinations of the teams, because, when the chips are down and the studio red light is on, and an awkward mechanical situation confronts the player, being able to meet the challenge successfully is the greatest boost for self-confidence, assurance, reputation, and of course the ego. It only has to happen once to make all the hours of practice and hard work very worthwhile and absolutely unforgetable.

I know how hard it is to work hours and hours on almost impossible problems. I also know that when this moment of truth arrives, it can be very frightening, because, all those many hours of work are going to be put to the acid test, now the player must "sink" or "swim" — if the latter prevails, all of those hours of hard work suddenly turn to "pure gold" —

GENERAL REMARKS

Always practice the difficult mechanical situations in complete privacy. There should be just one pair of ears listening to the results, yours. If there is another pair of ears present, you are performing. When performing, continuity and smoothness must prevail —

ARTICULATED 6THS

MAJOR AND MINOR

ARTICULATED 6THS

MAJOR AND MINOR

THIS VARIATION EXAMPLE CAN BE FINGERED MANY WAYS AND PLAYED IN MANY LOCATIONS - EXPERIMENT - CREATE OTHER VARIATIONS - CONTINUE THRU THE CYCLE OF 5THS

CHAPTER 3
STAGGER CONCEPT

THE STAGGER CONCEPT GENERAL REMARKS

Studying all of the many scale patterns may seem boring and needless. But without them intelligent improvisation is impossible.

Playing tunes/compositions may seem more satisfying, but without the various scale and arpeggio patterns, the musical chemistry of the compositions cannot be fully evaluated or understood clearly. In other words, you like the compositions, but you don't clearly know why, and that makes you a follower instead of a creator — as has been stated before: "Luck won't do it, and ignorance can't —

Chords are very much like chameleons, they can mean many many things, it all depends on when, where, and how, they are used —

BASIC EXPLANATION

The principle of the stagger concept is based on the use of the natural tones/steps of the scales, (any scale) major or minor. Used together in varying relationships and positions to each other to form chord voicings.

The purpose of the stagger concept is to be able to trace various voicings and relate them to the scales, and in so doing find all of the relatives of those voicings — the results are always interesting and very informative. Here is a good basic example:

When the lower "C" in this "C" chord is staggered one step down, the "C" scale to "B" voicing becomes a "C" major seventh with the seventh in the bass.

All of the relatives of this stagger can be traced by merely freezing the voicing, and then move the locked voicing down the scale while making sure that every voice follows the natural tones of the scale — the top voice must go from "C" down to "C" — the next voice must go from "G" to "G" — the next must go from "E" to "E" and the bottom voice must go from "B" to "B" —

The result of the one note stagger produces some "old friend" chords, such as the sixth step, fifth step, and of course, the third step, which is the first four strings of the open tuning:

• 1 7 6 5 4 3 2 1

It may seem at first, that the beginning "C" chord was altered, but it was not altered. Staggering is not altering; here is the proof: If the scale begins on the third step, (the open tuning step) the "C" chord with the "B" in the bass becomes a natural product of the open tuning — when the lower "C" is staggered one step down the scale, the open tuning becomes a product of the stagger — the product of staggering just one note.

The word "stagger" was chosen, because it most graphically describes what is actually happening to the normal notations. It has nothing to do with wobbling, or unsteady motion.

In the learning stage, staggering should be done mechanically, (visually) until the principle becomes familiar and logically accepted — this is most easily achieved by numbering 1/2 inch wide strips of paper from 1 to 15 evenly spaced and identical in length, then start numbers 1 to 7 under each 8, ending with number 1 under each 15 —

Quite naturally, all of the "ones" represent the tonic of the key, (any key) the upper numbers represent the continuous interval — example.

1	2	3	4	5	6	7	8	9	10	11	12	13	14	15
							1	2	3	4	5	6	7	1

When working with three voices, use three strips, four voices four strips etc. The numbers can be extended for wider range if necessary.

When the strips are placed directly one above the other there is no stagger, no chordal voicing, just unisons as the example shows:

1	2	3	4	5	6	7	8	9	etc.
							1	2	
1	2	3	4	5	6	7	8	9	
							1	2	
1	2	3	4	5	6	7	8	9	
							1	2	

(The stagger strips are read vertically)

When the strips are staggered one step each, successively, the first vertical reading is; tonic, second, third — EXAMPLE:

1	2	3	4	5	6	7	8	9		
							1	2		
	1	2	3	4	5	6	7	8	9 etc.	
								1	2	
		1	2	3	4	5	6	7	8	9
									1	2

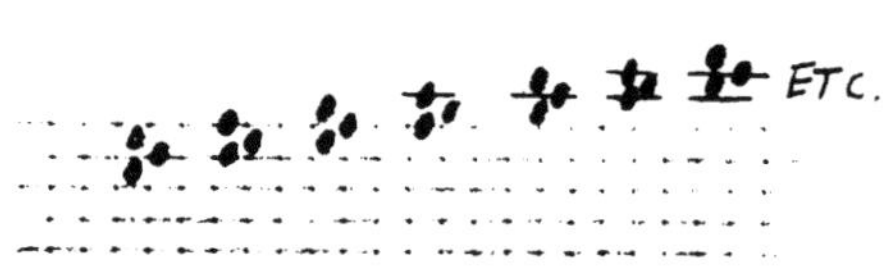

The three note vertical readings are now ready for running the scale — this stagger is now locked — the first full reading becomes the first step of the stagger —

Inversions of the first step = C D E

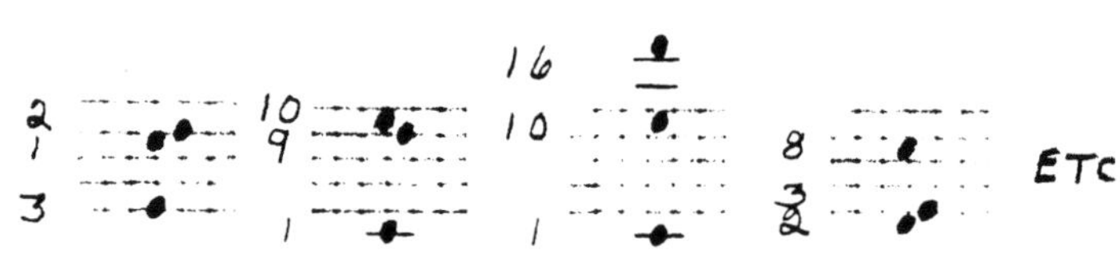

When the strips are staggered two steps each, successively, the first reading is; tonic, third, fifth, EXAMPLE:

				V								
1	2	3	4	5	6	7	8	9				
							1	2				
		1	2	3	4	5	6	7	8	9 etc.		
									1	2		
				1	2	3	4	5	6	7	8	9
											1	2

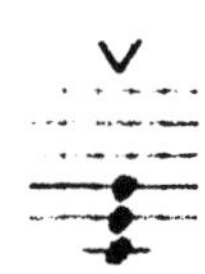

Staggering the strips two steps produces "root" inversion triads — whoch are sometimes called "third inversions" —

When the top strip is staggered two more steps, the first vertical reading becomes; which is a "C" major 7th, or, "A" minor 9th

The first inversion tonic triad would read this way;

```
                     V
1  2  3  4  5  6  7  8  9
                     1  2
         1  2  3  4  5  6  7  8  9 etc.
                              1  2
               1  2  3  4  5  6  7  8  9
                                    1  2
```

If the upper two voices were staggered one step up, the reading would be;

```
                        V
1  2  3  4  5  6  7  8  9
                     1  2
         1  2  3  4  5  6  7  8  9 etc.
                              1  2
                  1  2  3  4  5  6  7  8  9
                                       1  2
```

One to four voices:

```
            V
1  2  3  4  5  6  7  8  9
                     1  2
   1  2  3  4  5  6  7  8  9
                        1  2 etc.
      1  2  3  4  5  6  7  8  9
                           1  2
         1  2  3  4  5  6  7  8  9
                              1  2
```

Four voices:

```
                               V
          1  2  3  4  5  6  7  8  9 10 11 12 13 14 15
                               1  2  3  4  5  6  7  1
             1  2  3  4  5  6  7  8  9 10 11 12 13 14 15
                                  1  2  3  4  5  6  7  1
                         1  2  3  4  5  6  7  8  9 10 11 12 13 14 15
                                              1  2  3  4  5  6  7  1
                   1  2  3  4  5  6  7  8  9 10 11 12 13 14 15
                                     1  2  3  4  5  6  7  1
```

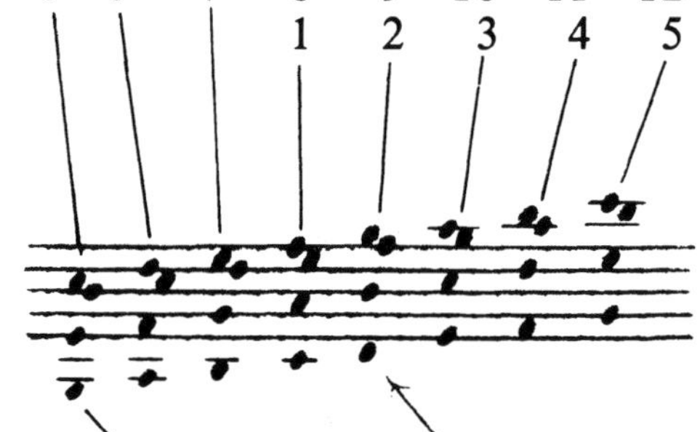

Notice where this "old friend" came from, the others are its relatives

```
                                                   V
1  2  3  4  5  6  7  8  9 10 11 12 13 14 15
                     1  2  3  4  5  6  7  1
   1  2  3  4  5  6  7  8  9 10 11 12 13 14 15
                        1  2  3  4  5  6  7  1
               1  2  3  4  5  6  7  8  9 10 11 12 13 14 15
                                 1  2  3  4  5  6  7  1
                           1  2  3  4  5  6  7  8  9 10 11 12 13 14 15
                                                 1  2  3  4  5  6  7  1
```

The lower example shows the overall interval, which is an eveventh —

The overall interval is not necessary when the stagger is broken down this way:

The lowest note is the fifth of the key, "G" — the note above the "G" is the third "E" — the note above that is the seventh "B" — the note above the "B" is the tonic 1 - 8 ——

GENERAL REMARKS

As has been mentioned, in using the stagger principle any chord can be traced and therefore related to some scale, and in the process "old friend" chords show up, chords that all players know regardless of how long they've been playing. Only now the player will have the advantage of knowing where the voicing has been, where it is at the moment (in the scale) and where it is going, or where it can go ——

These "old friend" chords take on a new dimension, a new look, and most importantly, a new respect.

Harmonically, this provides a better, deeper understanding of voicing, voice leading, and the relationships of the notes to one another.

Voices in a harmonized passage, using this line of thought actually become more like individual lines, rather than just block harmony.

By experimenting with the concept carefully, many new and different relationships can be found. The experiments can produce some rather surprising voicings, but now they will relate to each other and make harmonic sense continuity-wise.

Starting a scale with a very common voicing can produce some surprises as has been shown before, but they may not necessarily be new or unusual. That is not the point. The point is, that the entire family of the beginning chord is identified, and now thought of as belonging to the common beginning voicing.

A chord that has been staggered, can become the base for further staggering, and then that stagger can be staggered, etc., etc. ——

Experiment with all kinds of voicings open and closed. All staggers can be compounded progressively; in other words, when all of the tones have been staggered once, stagger them again, and again etc. ——

Stagger the notes up, and/or down, they can be in mixed order, parallel, contrary, any direction, but make sure to "freeze" the voicing interval-wise when it is taken through scales.

A tonic voicing, or first step of a scale can be staggered and re-staggered and still be thought of, and still be, the first step of the scale.

EXAMPLE:

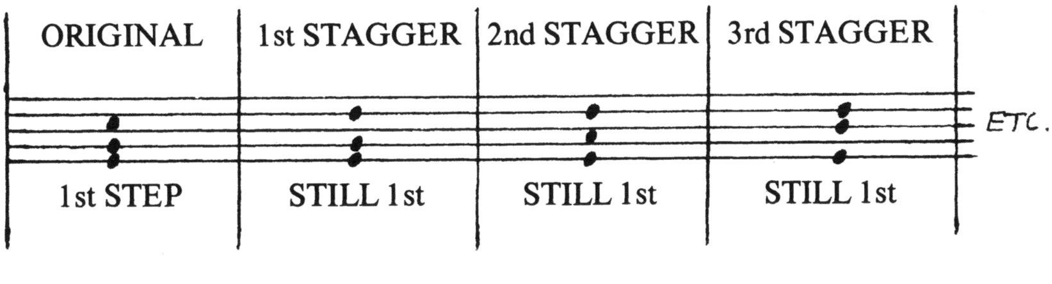

The third of the key "E" is dominating; that is why the first stagger is still the first step even though it does not contain the key note "C" —

Notice that when simple basic staggers are employed, the names/symbols change quite a bit. Here are three examples using just the three first steps of the "C" scale in first inversion triads.

By staggering one voice at a time, just one step up the scale, notice what happens to the symbols on the second and third steps;

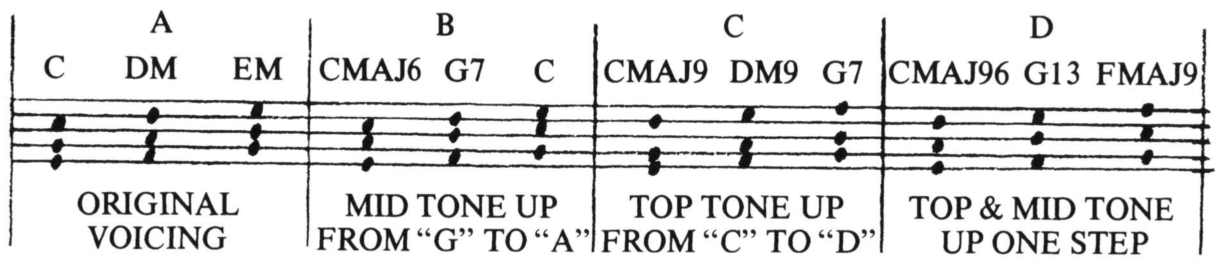

To trace the relatives of voicings, the basic procedure is as follows:

Let's use this common voicing of a "G" seventh as an example 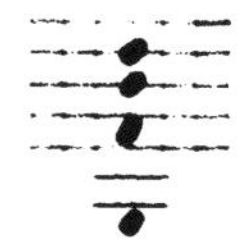

Now let's stagger the "D" a half tone down to "D" flat 

The lower three voices describe an open "G" seventh chord (the dominant seventh of "C" —)

The upper three voices enharmonically describe a "D" flat seventh chord which is the dominant seventh of "G" flat —

We now have four notes that describe two differently voiced seventh chords in two different keys:

The "G" seventh belongs to the "C" scale —

The "D" flat seventh belongs to the "G" flat scale —

Mathematically the two keys are as far apart as possible, "G" flat is right in the middle of the chromatic "C" octave as the example shows:

6 Chromatic steps either direction arrive at G♭ —
It's exactly in the middle of the octave

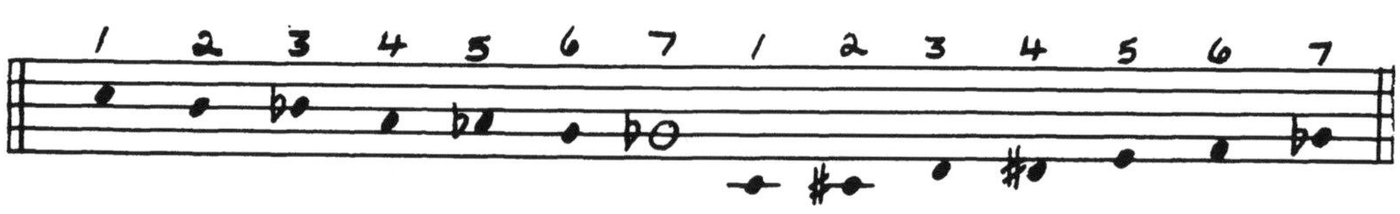

A — All four notes related to "C" make a "G" seventh chord with the flatted fifth on top —

All four notes related to "G" flat make a "D" flat seventh chord with the flatted fifth on the bottom (in the bass) ——

(3 BASIC EXAMPLES)

The upper voices can be placed in minor modes while keeping the bass in major. The lower voice can be placed in minor modes while keeping the upper voices in major, etc. experiment, mix them, here are a few examples:

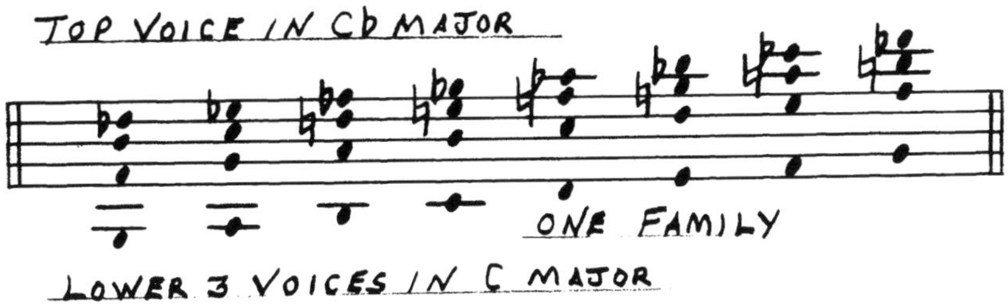

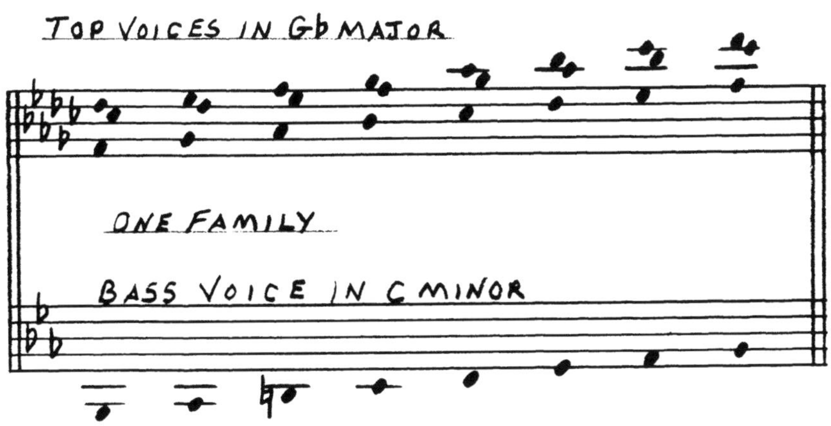

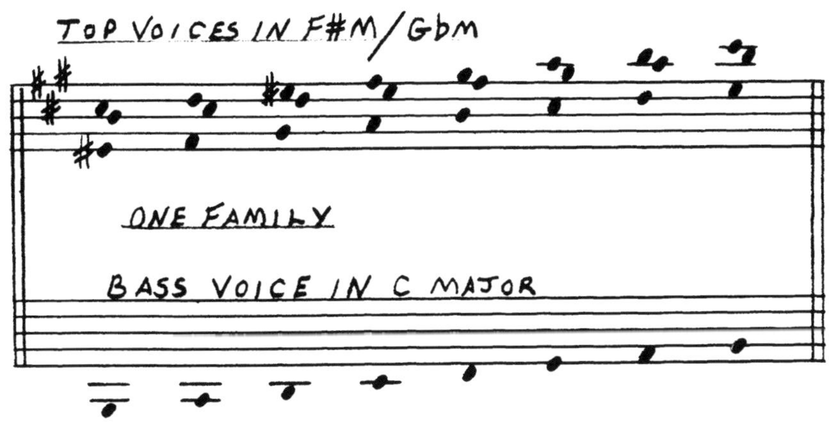

Each voice singly, or in pairs, trios, can be placed in major and minors, mixed major and minors etc.

For instance; top voice major, lower voices minor — upper and lower voice

Minor, middle voices in major etc. — employ mixed minors also.

Always freeze the experimental voicings by writing them out for one octave, play them over and over again and analyze the results carefully, methodically, and of course endeavor to remember the chemistry of the keys and modes involved, also experiment with mixtures of all the different keys.

The following three examples clearly demonstrate how much simple staggers can affect basic harmonic notation.

In the first bar of each example, the lower three notes represent an "A" minor second inversion triad with the middle tone "A" staggered one step up the scale to "B" — then the frozen voicing is taken down the scale. The lower three voices remain the same in each example.

In example one, the key note "A" is added above the staggered triad and then descends down the scale.

In example two, the top voice is staggered one step down the scale, thus beginning on "G" sharp, the seventh step of the scale.

In example three, the entire upper voice of example two is staggered one half tone down — in other words, the top line begins on the seventh step of the "G" sharp minor/"A" flat minor scale.

STAGGER CONCEPT

STAGGER EXAMPLES

MAJOR AND MINOR

ADD A♮ FOR MELODIC MINOR

CM

1
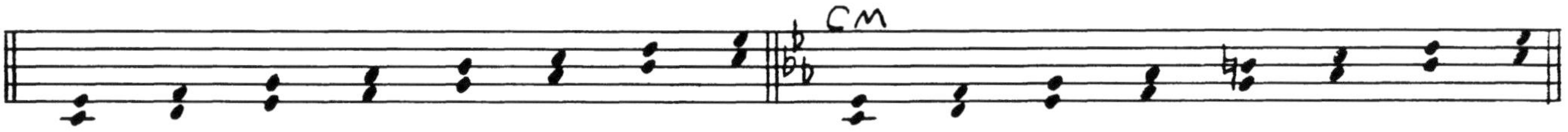

2
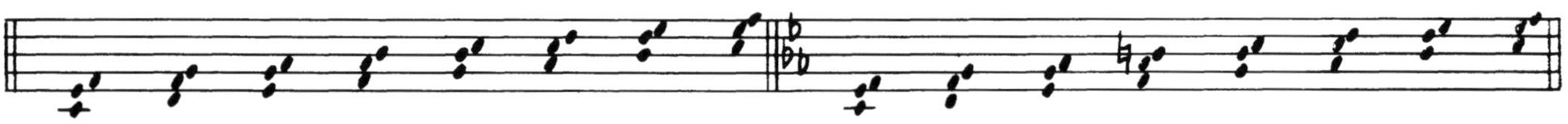

3

4

5
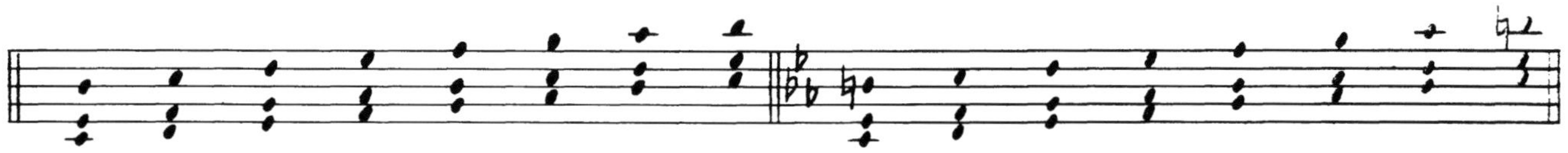

6
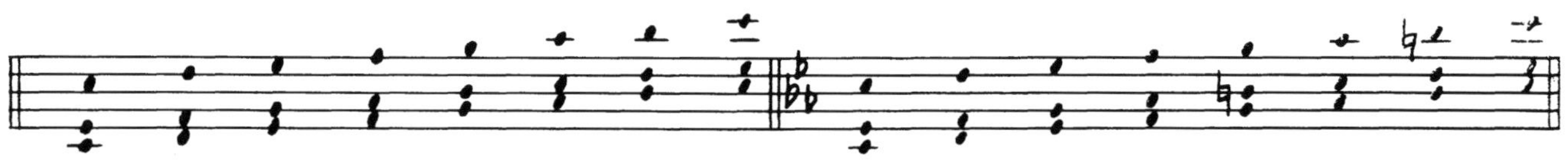

7

8

9

10

ADD A♮ FOR MELODIC MINOR
CM
11
12
13
14
15
16
17
18
19

ADD A♮ FOR MELODIC MINOR
CM
20
21
22
23

24

Number 25 in major requires quite long finger spreads — 25 in minor requires even longer spreads, however, try to play them both. If they are too long, 25 A & B contain the very same harmonic information and notation, except that the notes are sounded in arpeggio form.

25

25 A

25 B

26

27

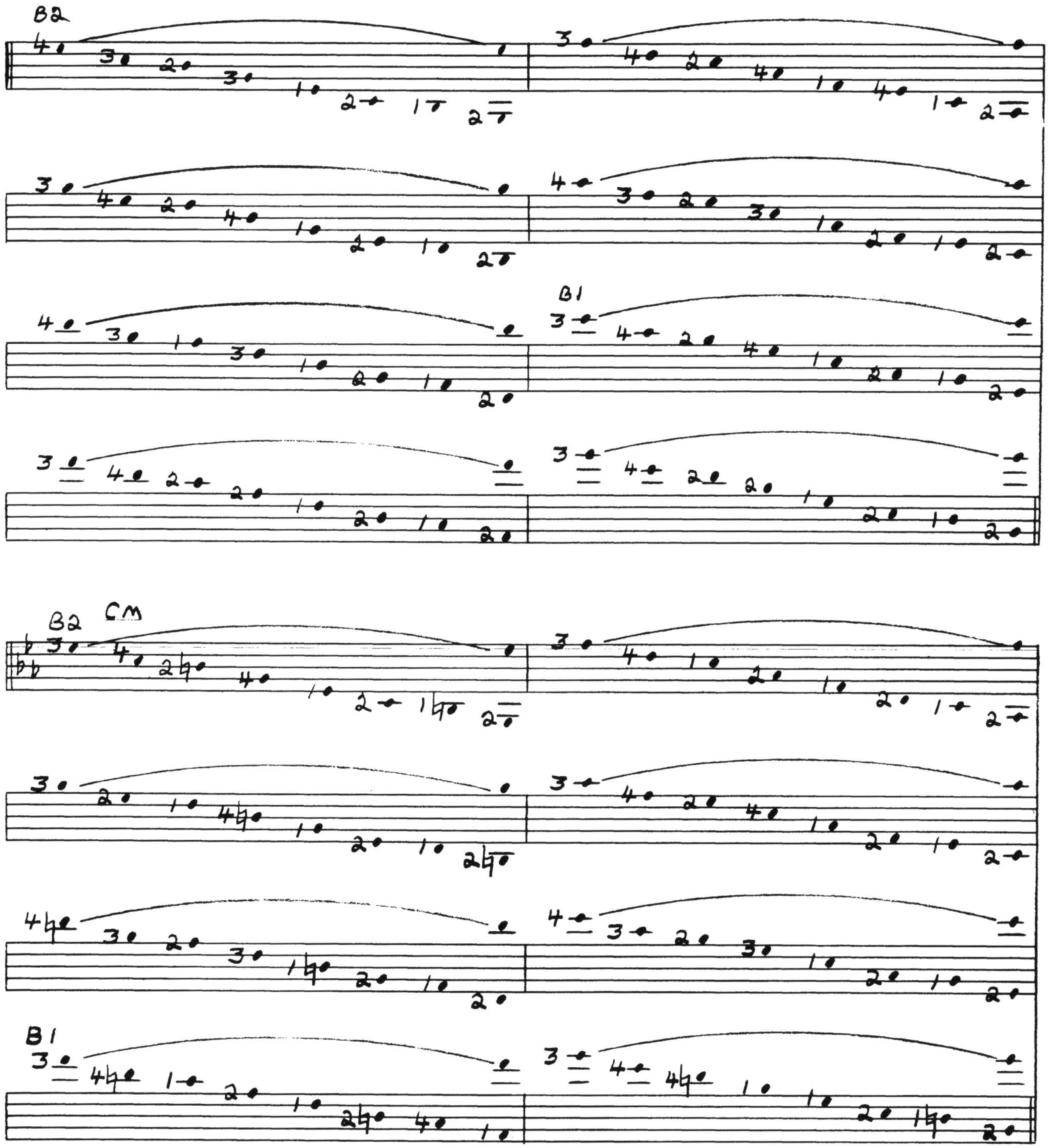

STAGGER EXAMPLES

MAJOR AND MINOR

28

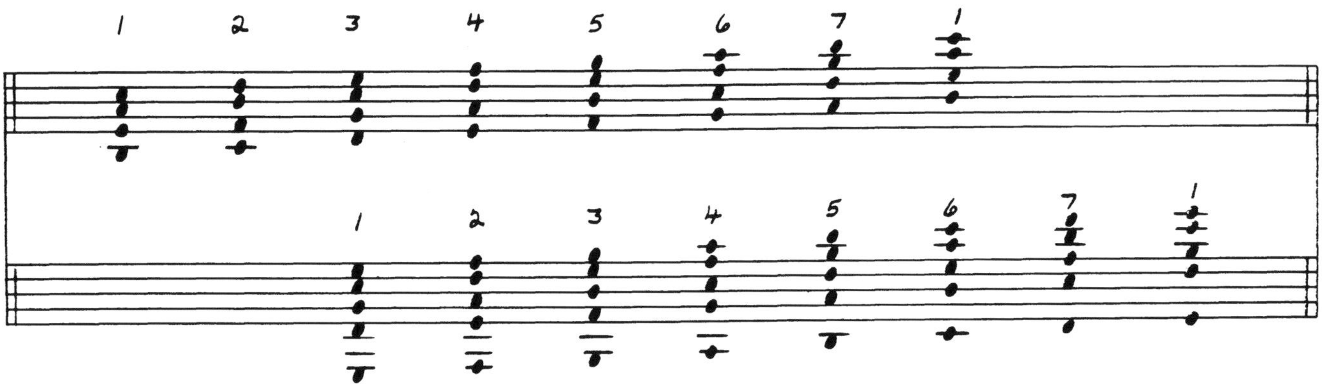

29

30

31

STAGGER EXAMPLES

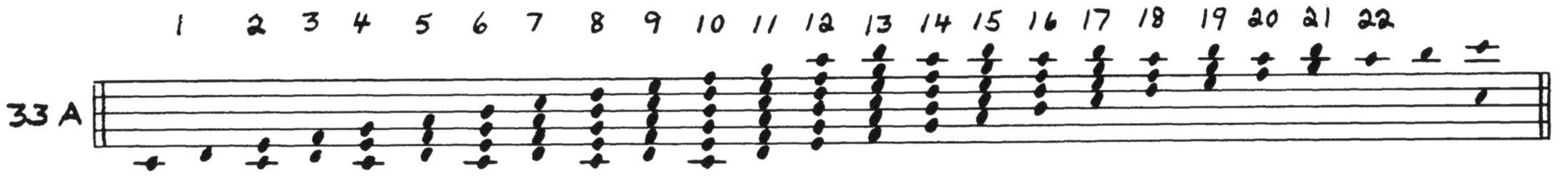

ALL THE VOICES IN THE ABOVE EXAMPLE CAN BE PLAYED AS SHOWN BELOW – MAJOR AND MINOR

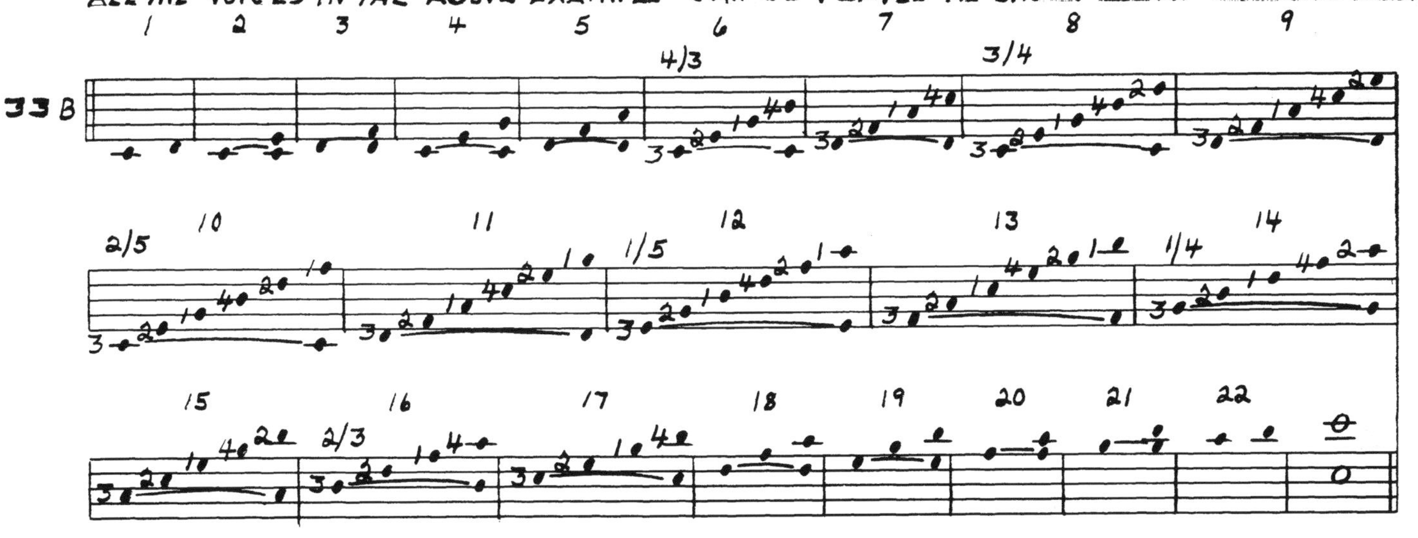

BAR 10 EXTENDED

BAR 10 MINOR VARIATION – ALWAYS TAKE ADVANTAGE OF THE POSSIBLE TIES FOR SMOOTHNESS

USED AS A RESOLUTION

STAGGER EXAMPLES

MAJOR AND MINOR

34

STAGGER—

TRIAD VOICES SUPER AND SUB- CONTRARY MOTION—CHROMATIC UPPER LINE- MULTI VOICE MOTION-

THE STAGGER CONCEPT GENERAL REMARKS

The question may arise, "What has all this got to do with playing the guitar? —" Answer; it has this to do with playing the guitar, or any instrument:

The products of the stagger concept are usually uncommon voicings, especially for the guitar.

They require unfamiliar fingerings most of the time because their shapes are unusual.

The end result is that the information learned from staggering a variety of voicings, note-by-note, is very useful harmonically. The fingering necessary to produce the resultant voicings becomes very useful gymnastically.

As has been mentioned before, a guitarists hands, to be well rounded, must be ready for the "unusual" — the uncommon situations.

CHAPTER 4
ODD AGAINST EVEN

These studies are meant to be tools to build musical structures. How to use them must be dictated by one's ear and taste, sense of proportion and balance. The ear knows pleasing sounds, and the combinations of sound.
It must never be said that "this" is the only way to do it. However, I do feel that with careful study these books can provide many of the ways to play difficult, complicated harmonics.

STRING CHART

EXPLANATION OF THE STRING SET SYMBOLS:

A vertical or angled line thus– / –means "Set"—
The number in front of it is the set number—
The number after it indicates the number of strings employed—
Example:
When the 1st-2nd-3rd-strings are employed the symbol is:
1/3—The first set of three–etc.
When the 1st-2nd-3rd-4th-strings are employed the symbol is:
1/4—The 1st set of four–etc.

THE BROKEN AND THE DIVIDED SETS:

Example:
When the 1st-2nd-4th-strings are employed (skipping the 3rd string) it is termed a broken set—the symbol is:
1/B3—The first set of broken three–etc.
When the order is reversed, (skipping the 2nd instead of the 3rd string) the word "broken" is used first, thus:
B1/3—The broken first set of three–etc.

When the 1st-2nd-4th-5th-strings are employed it is termed a divided set—the symbol is:
D1/4—The divided first set of four–etc.
When the 1st-3rd-5th-strings are employed the symbol is:
1/D3—The first set of divided three—and so on—
When the 1st-4th-strings are employed the symbol is:
A 1—
When the 2nd-5th-strings are employed the symbol is:
A 2—etc.
When the 1st-5th-strings are employed the symbol is:
B 1—etc.

NOTE
A symbol for the 1st-3rd-4th-6th-strings is not necessary because it would encompass all of the strings, therefore, the very notation dictates where and on what strings the notes are located.

STRING SET CHART

SYMBOLS:—STRINGS EMPLOYED—

1/2—1st-2nd-
2/2—2nd-3rd-
3/2—3rd-4th-
4/2—4th-5th-
5/2—5th-6th-

1/3—1st-2nd-3rd-
2/3—2nd-3rd-4th-
3/3—3rd-4th-5th-
4/3—4th-5th-6th-

1/4—1st-2nd-3rd-4th-
2/4—2nd-3rd-4th-5th-
3/4—3rd-4th-5th-6th-

1/5—1st-2nd-3rd-4th-5th-
2/5—2nd-3rd-4th-5th-6th-

THE BROKEN AND DIVIDED SETS:

1/B2—1st-3rd-
2/B2—2nd-4th-
3/B2—3rd-5th-
4/B2—4th-6th-

1/B3—1st-2nd-4th-
2/B3—2nd-3rd-5th-
3/B3—3rd-4th-6th-

B1/3—1st-3rd-4th-
B2/3—2nd-4th-5th-
B3/3—3rd-5th-6th-

1/B4—1st-2nd-3rd-5th-
2/B4—2nd-3rd-4th-6th-

B1/4—1st-3rd-4th-5th-
B2/4—2nd-4th-5th-6th-
1D/3—1st-2nd-5th-
2D/3—2nd-3rd-6th-

1/D3—1st-3rd-5th-
2/D3—2nd-4th-6th-

D1/3—1st-4th-5th-
D2/3—2nd-5th-6th-

D1/4—1st-2nd-4th-5th-
D2/4—2nd-3rd-5th-6th-

A1—1st-4th-
A2—2nd-5th-
A3—3rd-6th-

B1—1st-5th-
B2—2nd-6th-

01—1st-6th-

ODD AGAINST EVEN

The purposes of this chapter are many fold. One of them is to learn how to divide the mind into segments and still keep track of those segments; in other words, it is developing the knack of being able to focus the mind clearly on two different time elements simultaneously, by dividing the mind in half.

Odd against even means that in a given time frame, (bar lines) two opposing rhythms must work together as friends smoothly while each one keeps it's identity.

For instance, two does not divide evenly into three, nor does three divide into two, but in music it has to be done. The odd one has to go a little faster or slower in order to fit into the time frame. It's like having to make friends out of enemies.

A triplet, for instance is squeezed into an even number — three quarter notes must take up the same space as two in the time frame etc.

The work material on the following pages is not really hard, it just requires some quiet concentration. The examples are not marked because the fingerings and mechanisms have been shown in past studies. Logical fingering is necessary of course, but in these studies the focus is on the compatibility of the opposing time elements.
They will fight each other of course, but it must become a friendly, loving, smooth performance.

Three against two and four against three are very interesting highly useable opposing beats.

Five against four is not as common as the other two, but is very useable and intersting as the examples show.
It was included because the opposition requires complete concentration, and it also provides good mental and physical exercise. Five against four provides a better understanding of the vernier principle involved, and in so doing helps all the other opposing time elements, values, syncopation, etc.

The following examples are merely basic suggestions and only show a little bit of the vast potential and usefulness, not only in the music itself, but in the mental and physical discipline this process can develop.

Experiment with all kinds of voicings and harmonic structures, employing the three pairs of opposing beats shown in the examples — run them forward, backwards, upside down, etc.

EXPLANATION OF THE TIMING BLOCKS —

The vertical lines dividing the boxes in each block indicate the exact location, time-wise, of the beats in the time signatures that oppose each other.

All opposing timing of beats can be blocked out in this manner, the boxes provide a clear visual picture of the opposition. By sliding a ruler vertically across the blocks at a steady, even, slow speed, the actual placement of the beats opposing each other can be visually read (heard mentally) and converted to sound.

The exact placement of the beats may not be correct in the beginning, and therefore not sound right, but by working very carefully with them they should, after a time, smooth out quite a bit. When this moment arrives, the realization will be that the effort was well worth the end result, and that the study time was well spent.

Syncopation of all kinds will become much easier to understand and play by having worked with studies such as these.

The timing of the opposing beats are blocked out this way —

The notation will be written this way — The lower 2 staves show the actual time signatures —

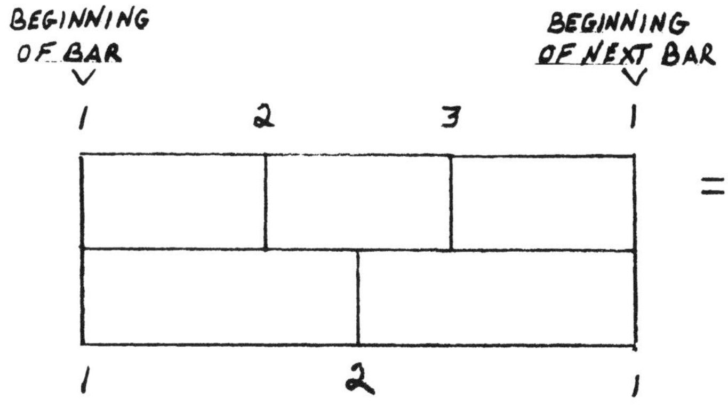

3 AGAINST 2

2 AGAINST 3

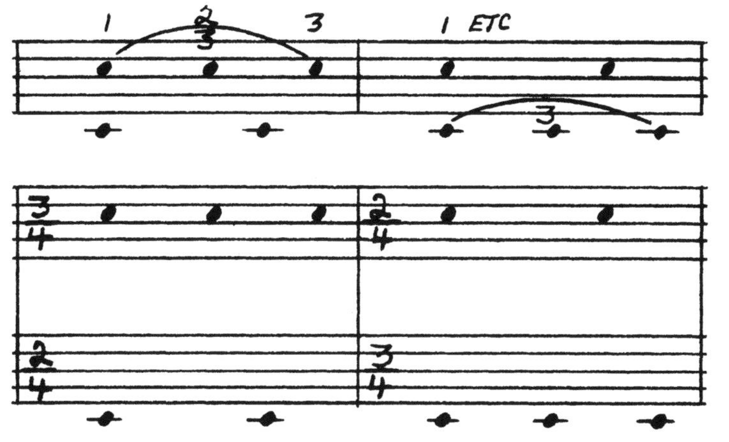

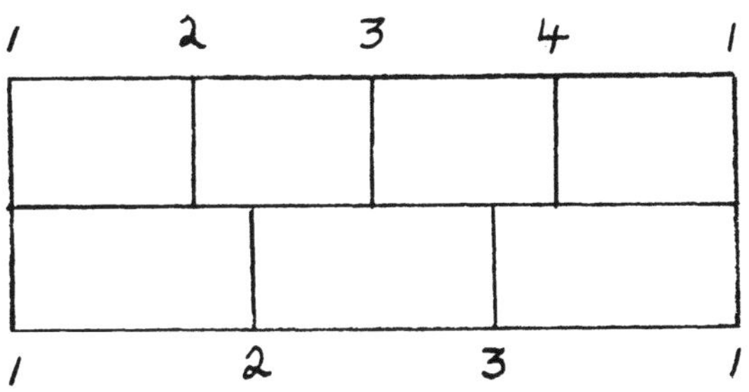

4 AGAINST 3

3 AGAINST 4

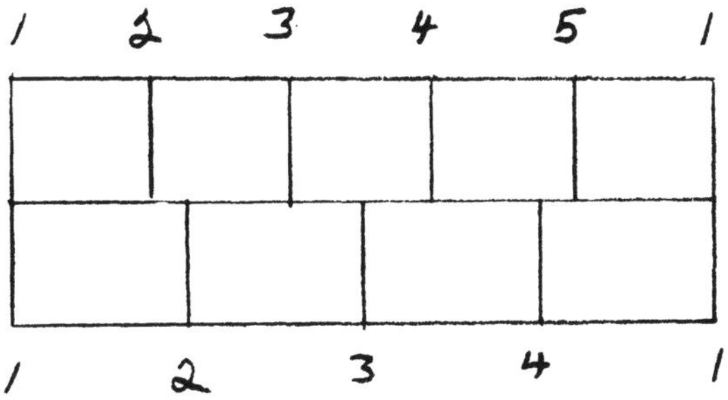

5 AGAINST 4

4 AGAINST 5

The blocks were first laid out in a string of boxes based on the common denominator of both time signatures as these examples show. Then they were refined by eliminating the extra vertical lines. This process locates the exact position of the opposing beats. All opposing time values (beats) can be blocked out in boxes, and evaluated mechanically this way.

3 AGAINST 2 — (The Common Denominator = 6)

6 Boxes Each

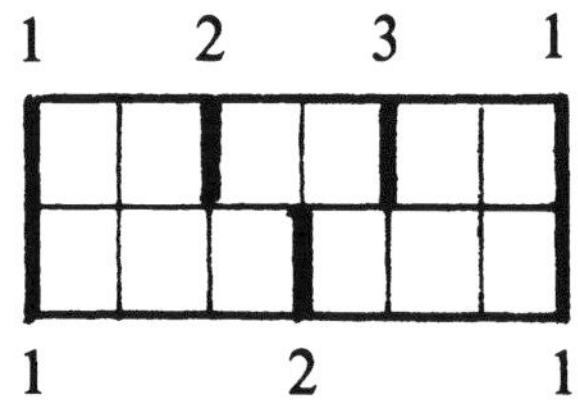

4 AGAINST 3 — (The Common Denominator = 12)

12 Boxes Each

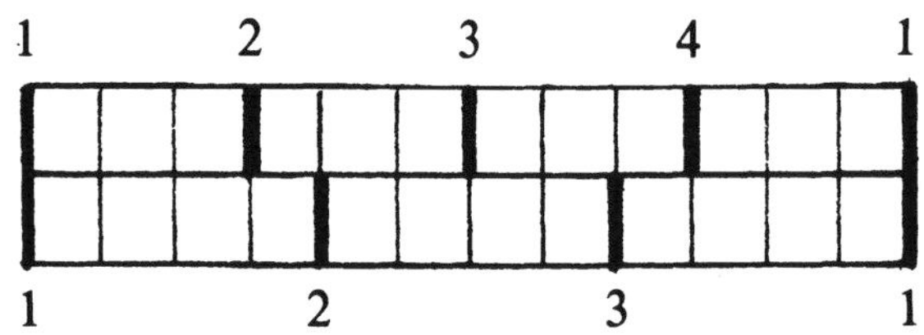

5 AGAINST 4 — (The Common Denominator = 20)

20 Boxes Each

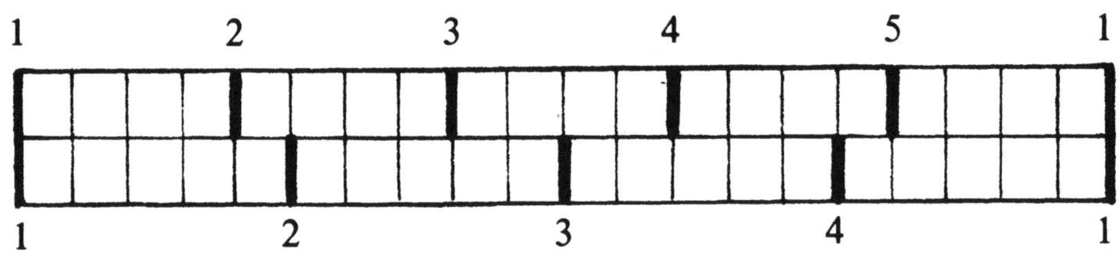

Using just numbers:

```
                  V       V       V     |V
3 AGAINST 2 —     1   2   3   4   5   6 |1  etc.
                  Λ           Λ          Λ

                V         V         V          V          |V
4 AGAINST 3 —   1  2  3   4  5  6   7  8   9   10  11  12 |1  etc.
                Λ            Λ             Λ              |Λ

5 AGAINST 4 —
V         V           V              V              V                |V
1 2 3 4   5 6 7 8     9 10 11 12     13 14 15 16    17 18 19 20      |1  etc.
Λ           Λ            Λ                  Λ                        |Λ
```

The same three examples now presented similar to drum beats:

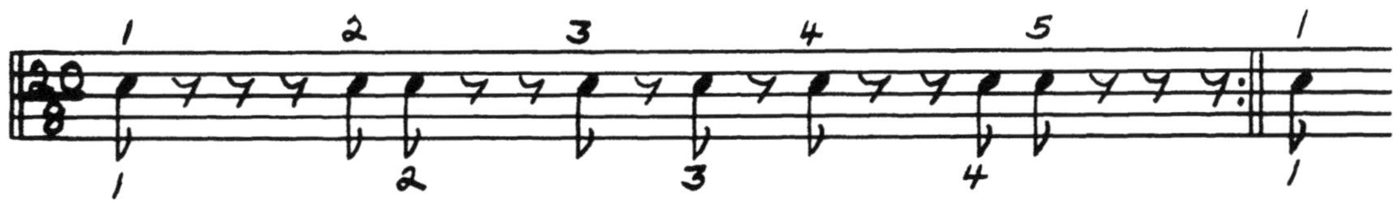

Here is another way to lay out the opposing beats using numbers:

```
              V     V     V
3 AGAINST 2 — 1  2  3  4  5  6
              Λ        Λ

              V        V        V        V
4 AGAINST 3 — 1  2  3  4  1  2  3  4  1  2  3  4
              Λ           Λ           Λ

              V           V           V           V           V
5 AGAINST 4 — 1  2  3  4  5  1  2  3  4  5  1  2  3  4  5  1  2  3  4  5
              Λ              Λ              Λ              Λ
```

The curved lines encompassing the odd beats must not be confused with, or, treated like tie lines. They merely bracket the odd groups of three and five — examples:

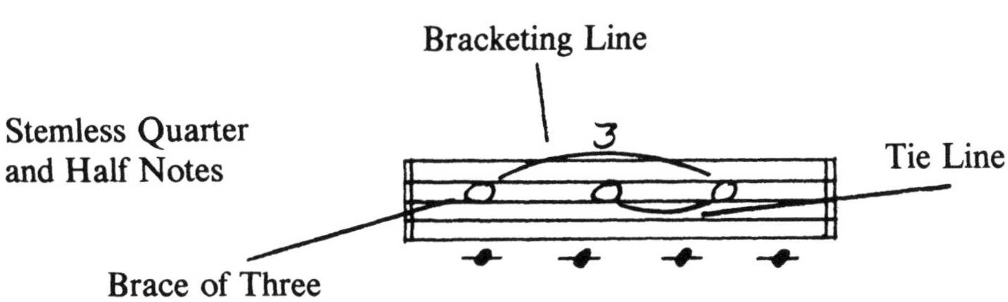

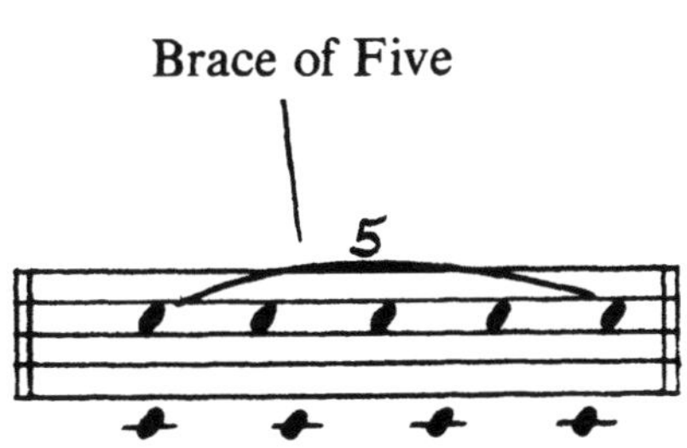

ODD AGAINST EVEN – EXAMPLES, 2 BARS EACH –

3 AGAINST 2 – APPLY TO SCALE STUDIES IN ALL VOICINGS – MINOR ALSO

ODD AGAINST EVEN

3 AGAINST 2

KEEP IN MIND THAT A BAR LINE CANCELS PREVIOUS ACCIDENTALS

ODD AGAINST EVEN–
4 AGAINST 3–

ODD AGAINST EVEN
4 AGAINST 3

ODD AGAINST EVEN

4 AGAINST 3

ODD AGAINST EVEN –

5 AGAINST 4

GENERAL REMARKS

The player must be prepared to cope with the unknown. Especially the professional, but, he or she cannot cover all of the unknowns. They can prepare themselves by becoming familiar with "key" mechanisms and notations that will enable them to handle unfamiliar situations, mechanisms that require just slight modifications and adjustment — example: If the player is familiar with the diatonic and chromatic scales, any scale can be played.

CHAPTER 5
THE SATELLITE CONCEPT

These studies are meant to be tools to build musical structures. How to use them must be dictated by one's ear and taste, sense of proportion and balance. The ear knows pleasing sounds, and the combinations of sound.
It must never be said that "this" is the only way to do it. However, I do feel that with careful study these books can provide many of the ways to play difficult, complicated harmonics.

STRING CHART

EXPLANATION OF THE STRING SET SYMBOLS:

A vertical or angled line thus– / –means "Set"—
The number in front of it is the set number—
The number after it indicates the number of strings employed—
Example:
When the 1st-2nd-3rd-strings are employed the symbol is:
1/3—The first set of three–etc.
When the 1st-2nd-3rd-4th-strings are employed the symbol is:
1/4—The 1st set of four–etc.

THE BROKEN AND THE DIVIDED SETS:

Example:
When the 1st-2nd-4th-strings are employed (skipping the 3rd string) it is termed a broken set—the symbol is:
1/B3—The first set of broken three–etc.
When the order is reversed, (skipping the 2nd instead of the 3rd string) the word "broken" is used first, thus:
B1/3—The broken first set of three–etc.

When the 1st-2nd-4th-5th-strings are employed it is termed a divided set—the symbol is:
D1/4—The divided first set of four–etc.
When the 1st-3rd-5th-strings are employed the symbol is:
1/D3—The first set of divided three—and so on—
When the 1st-4th-strings are employed the symbol is:
A 1—
When the 2nd-5th-strings are employed the symbol is:
A 2—etc.
When the 1st-5th-strings are employed the symbol is:
B 1—etc.

NOTE
A symbol for the 1st-3rd-4th-6th-strings is not necessary because it would encompass all of the strings, therefore, the very notation dictates where and on what strings the notes are located.

STRING SET CHART

SYMBOLS:—STRINGS EMPLOYED—

1/2—1st-2nd-
2/2—2nd-3rd-
3/2—3rd-4th-
4/2—4th-5th-
5/2—5th-6th-

1/3—1st-2nd-3rd-
2/3—2nd-3rd-4th-
3/3—3rd-4th-5th-
4/3—4th-5th-6th-

1/4—1st-2nd-3rd-4th-
2/4—2nd-3rd-4th-5th-
3/4—3rd-4th-5th-6th-

1/5—1st-2nd-3rd-4th-5th-
2/5—2nd-3rd-4th-5th-6th-

THE BROKEN AND DIVIDED SETS:

1/B2—1st-3rd-
2/B2—2nd-4th-
3/B2—3rd-5th-
4/B2—4th-6th-

1/B3—1st-2nd-4th-
2/B3—2nd-3rd-5th-
3/B3—3rd-4th-6th-

B1/3—1st-3rd-4th-
B2/3—2nd-4th-5th-
B3/3—3rd-5th-6th-

1/B4—1st-2nd-3rd-5th-
2/B4—2nd-3rd-4th-6th-

B1/4—1st-3rd-4th-5th-
B2/4—2nd-4th-5th-6th-
1D/3—1st-2nd-5th-
2D/3—2nd-3rd-6th-

1/D3—1st-3rd-5th-
2/D3—2nd-4th-6th-

D1/3—1st-4th-5th-
D2/3—2nd-5th-6th-

D1/4—1st-2nd-4th-5th-
D2/4—2nd-3rd-5th-6th-

A1—1st-4th-
A2—2nd-5th-
A3—3rd-6th-

B1—1st-5th-
B2—2nd-6th-

01—1st-6th-

GENERAL REMARKS

Every step in a progression is an intermediate resolution —

SATELLITE CONCEPT

The satellite principle is based on a series of triplex tones —

Immediate one move resolution from any key to all keys —

Resolutions through the use of the "grande" arpeggio which is the diatonic scale less the fourth step —

THE SATELLITE CONCEPT GENERAL REMARKS

This concept is based on a series of three note chromatic units (triplex's) — The purpose of which is to provide a mental and physical approach to the chromatic scale, that ties all keys together in an interwoven manner similar to the links in a chain —

The triplex's overlap each other = 

When the concept is applied to the individual notes of the "grande arpeggio" immediate one move resolutions are possible from any key, to any key.

THE SATELLITE NOTE PRINCIPLE

The satellite principle, as the name suggests, has to do with a center or main note that is surrounded by two other notes; one of them one half tone below, and the other one half tone above.

This makes a group of three » half tone steps; the center note being the main note.

The closest notes to any given note, musically, and geographically are the notes one half tone above and below that given note. For example; the closest notes to "C" are C flat and C sharp — (and of course, enharmonically B and D flat). The satellite notes of "C" sharp are C natural and D — and so on through the chromatic scale.

The mental picture is that every note has these two satellite notes that enjoy a close intimate relationship with each center note.

In the application of this principle it doesn't matter which of the two notes is used first, the order is optional. One can also go from a lower satellite note to the upper one directly, and the reverse of course. The application of this principle is quite simple, however, the results are » not quite as simple.

The application thoughtline is that a note, or group of notes have a potential of movement around the actual notes being sounded. But before going more fully into the » actual work, I want to go into the concept in more detail using examples.

First, it is important to visualize the chromatic scale surrounded by the satellite notes — Example:

The satellite concept is intended to help train one to think in voice lines, rather than just block harmony and formations.

The satellite notes are always just one half tone away from the center/main note. To enjoy the position of immediate resolution they must be the closest notes, and always be in the position of leading tones. If they move more than a half tone away there would be a gap, and they would become intervals that no longer enjoy the close intimacy that allows them to be immediately resolvable, and always in a passing tone position no matter where they are. In other words, if "C" is the center note the satellite notes would not go beyond C flat and C sharp, but one must remember that the center note naturally can move anywhere, and in so moving will be followed and surrounded by two satellite notes. For instance: if "C" were moved to "F" sharp, "F" sharp would now become the center note and would be surrounded by F and G natural. Keep in mind that every notes has its satellites, therefore, two part harmony is involved with four satellites, three part harmony has six, etc. Also keep in mind that any satellite can become a center note, bearing it's own satellites.

The normal chromatic scale contains twelve steps that just touch each other like a series of circles side by side as shown in this example:

In this example using a triplex thoughtline, notice the interwoven overlap of the three triplex's.

In other words, every note is both center and satellite.

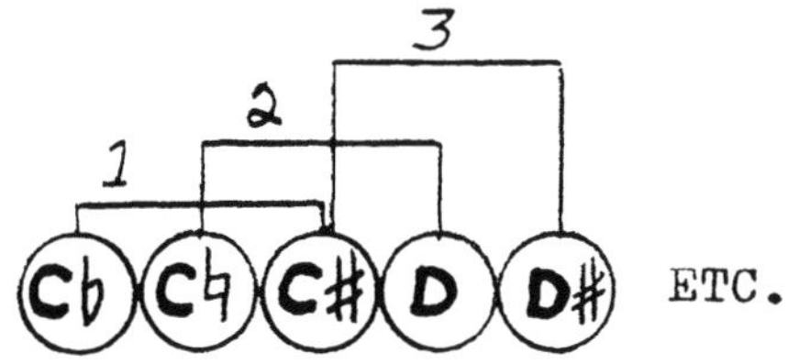

Think of the concept as having an interlaced appearance when two or more triplex' are involved.

Notice in the example below, that the center notes of the first three basic triplex' are shown as whole notes, and that by making the satellite notes centers of triplex', the basic three now become seven triplex' all interlaced and overlaping each other.

The next example is intended to point out, and make clear the fact that in the first three steps there are three "C" sharps. The thought line is, that in traveling just three chromatic steps, three "C" sharps have become involved on one angle and two whole tone steps (a major third) on the opposite angle — in other words, no motion one direction to semi advance motion the other.

C♭	C♮	C#
C♮	C#	D
C#	D	D#

The example below, shows the three basic triads as centers

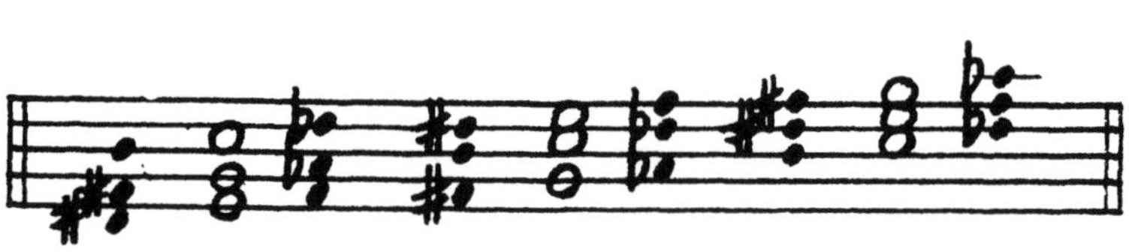

Satellites

The satellites can become centers, then the resulting satellites become centers and so on adinfinitum —

All scales, arpeggio's, harmonic structures become masses of tones with a vast potential of motion when thinking in satellite note terms, tones that can always be in flux, on the move, restless, like a sea of moving small notes that can at the same time be big notes all in motion — all placed one on top of the other like layers, while remaining logical and still maintaining their identities. In saying "small" and "big" notes, I'm referring to the momentary importance of a note, or notes — in other words, when a note, or a group of notes are in the immediate musical foreground they would be "big" and therefore important. As they recede into the background they may become small, and smaller, but, at the same time still be very important to the overall musical picture. The importance of any note can of course be melodic, harmonic, rhythmic, dynamic, or all four. Satellite notes can be thought of as leading tones, the lower one normal, the upper one inverted, but it's not inverted when related to the next higher triplex etc. They should be thought of as passing tones also.

GENERAL REMARKS

Using this concept in conjunction with the "grande" arpeggios of all the keys can provide many things when applied properly, such as:

Immediate resolution from any given key, to any of the others, in one move —

Smooth, subtle, voice leading in any or all of the lines employed. If the passage or progression contains let's say, four lines, the top line can be in motion, or the next line, or the next line, or the next. They can move seperately, or in pairs, or any combinations desired, in any direction. The lines can move in parallel, contrary, independant, or mixed motion, independant mixtures of all of them.

Taste, choice, and balance becomes the deciding factor.

Smooth, subtle, voice motion is not always easy to achieve, because the smoothness depends directly on the level of the players physical and mental dexterity, of course.

Common chords and progressions take on a new dimension and respect, when this concept is applied to them.

In the final analysis, the musicians basic tools are the scales and the first, second, and third inversion triads in all of the modes. All of the musical houses built, must come from them through the use of imagination, creativity, and work.

The beginning application of this concept is purposely kept quite simple. It starts with just two voices; a duo, moving one voice at a time through set patterns, as the examples show.

Bear in mind that each center/prime has two satellite notes, therefore, two voices have a potential of four satellites.

The examples begin with 2nd intervals on up to the 10th interval, but should be continued up to 11ths, 12ths, 13ths, 14ths etc.

These examples shot a basic pattern that is meant to be reversed and rearranged later on when the concept becomes familiar.

Use the examples as models, then make up other patterns — the more the better. Listen carefully to the resulting harmonic, structural, notational, and formational changes caused by the motion of the voices.

Later, apply the patterns shown, plus your own to various harmonic scales and progressions in all registers and keys.

The examples are in the key of "C" for the sake of clarity — quite naturally, the patterns will work well in many other harmonic situations.

Apply these patterns to the 2nd and 3rd inversions also. Experiment with many different voicings, open, closed, etc.

SATELLITE PRINCIPLE EXAMPLES

2NDS

UPPER VOICE ONLY | LOWER VOICE ONLY | PARALLEL MOTION | CONTRARY MOTION

3RDS

4THS

5THS

6THS

7THS

8THS

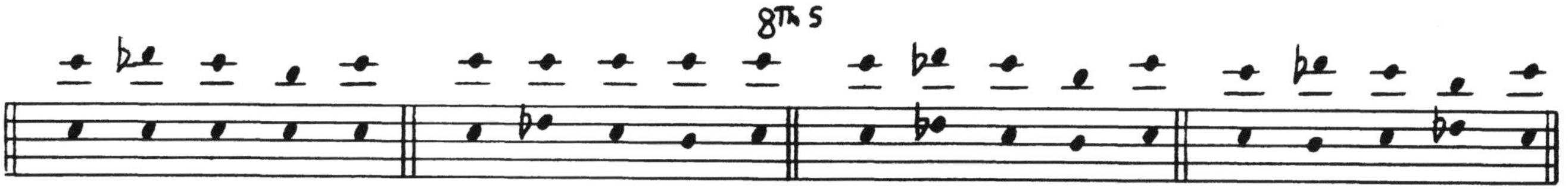

9THS

10THS

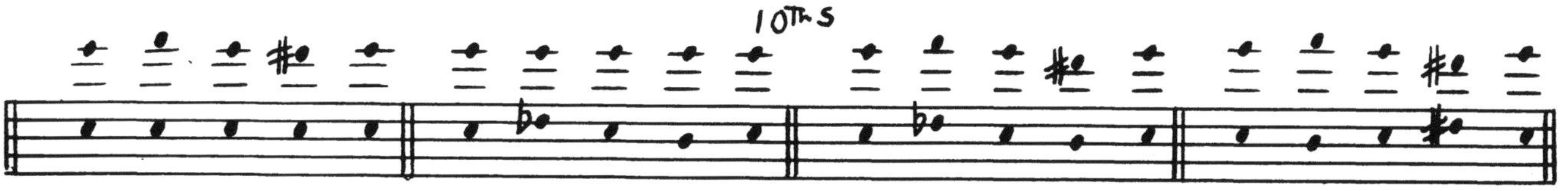

In these examples the three lines are completely independent —

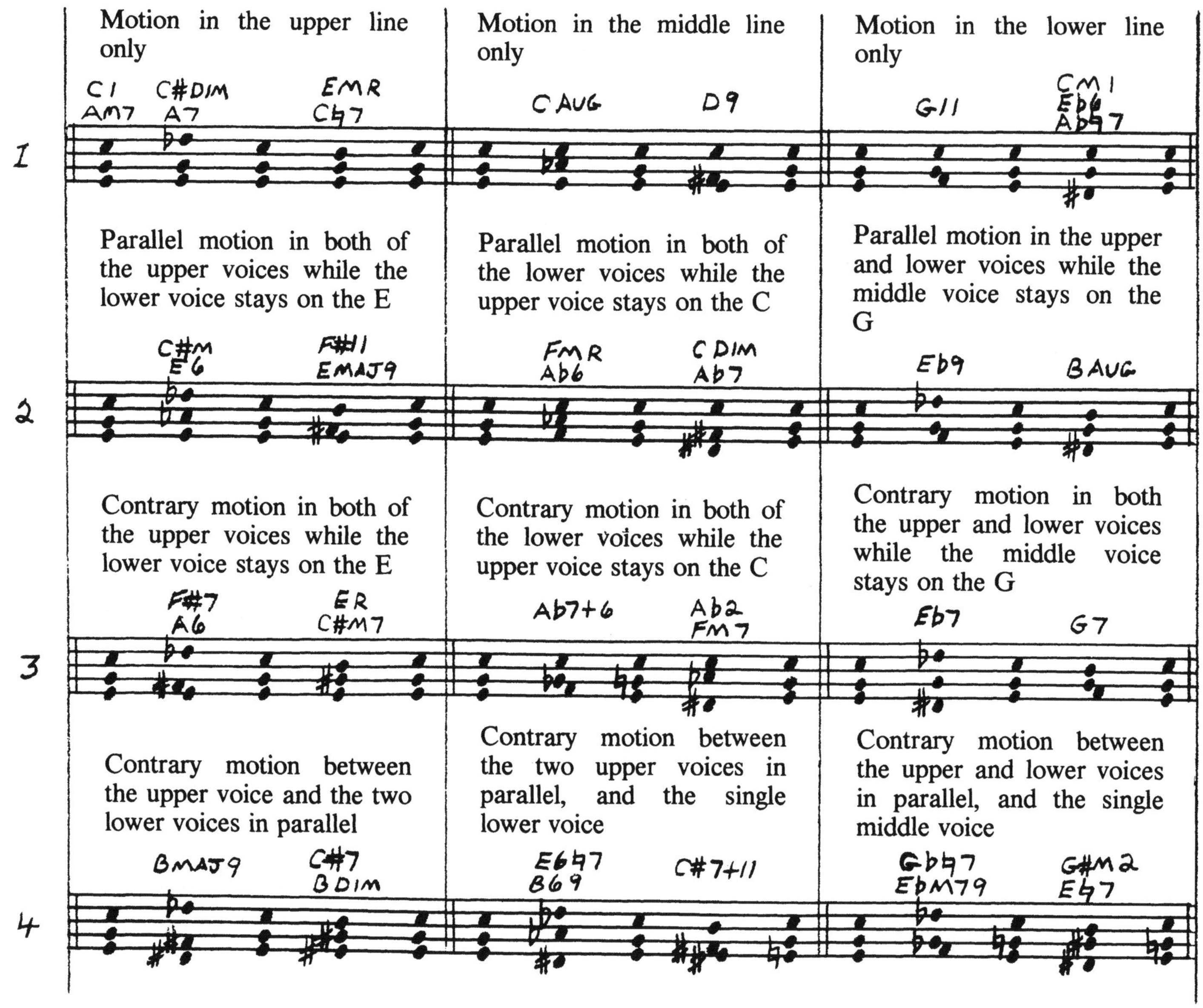

Use the patterns in the above examples to explore and experiment with harmonic situations of all kinds, and be aware of the notations and their appearance — think lines, lines, lines.

SATELLITE PRINCIPLE - LOWER LINE IS DIATONIC SCALE 3RD TO 3RD - MIDDLE LINE IS 1/2 TONE HIGH DOWN TO NORMAL - TOP LINE IS 1/2 TONE LOW UP TO NORMAL - EVEN NUMBERS ARE NORMAL

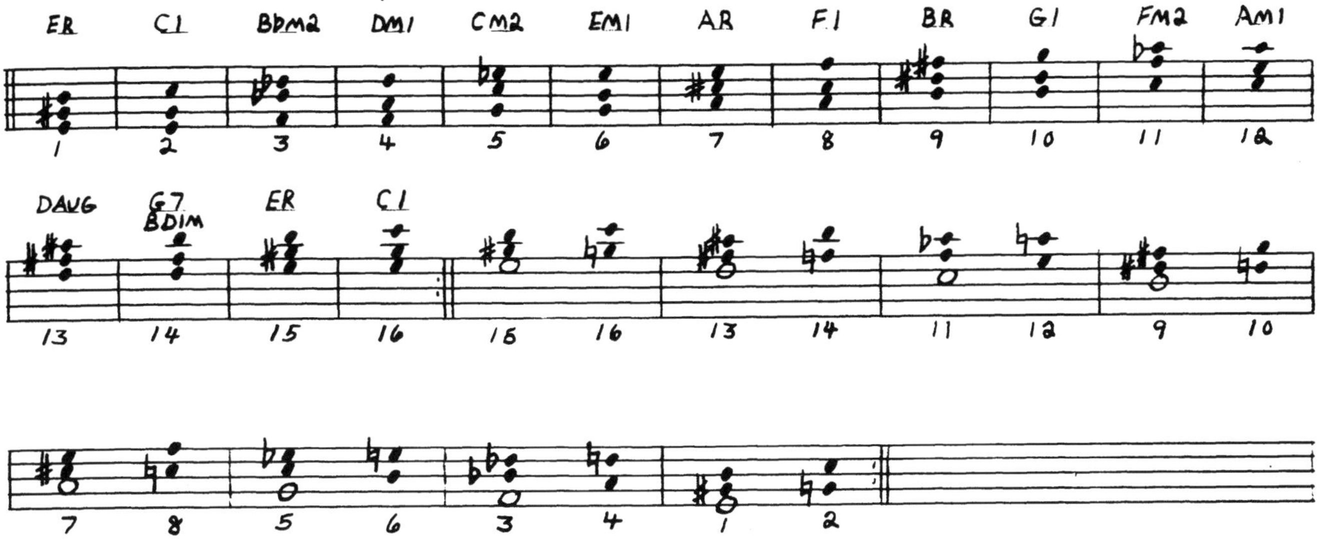

VARIATION

ANOTHER VARIATION USING A DIFFERENT HARMONIZATION - CHROMATIC LOWER LINE

IMMEDIATE RESOLUTION
GENERAL REMARKS

Think of a triplex as a little, small, tiny, chromatic scale that moves around freely, and with ease within the "big" overall chromatic scale — as the following example demonstrates —

SATELLITE PRINCIPLE EXAMPLES – PLAY BAR 1 OF EXAMPLE 1 - THEN BAR 1 OF EXAMPLE 2 ETC.

A SERIES OF TRIPLEX' ALL LINKED TOGETHER = 

EXAMPLE

1

2

EXAMPLES 1 AND 2 TOGETHER

3

IMMEDIATE RESOLUTION

In the following examples all keys are resolved one to the other in one smooth move.

None of the three voices in each example move more than a semi-tone up or down from the opening voicing; and of course the opening, or first notes in each example are centers. The satellite notes provide the smooth move and in being utilized, now become centers — chain reaction — the notes in the key being resolved to (2nd triad) now become centers. This mass of motion goes on and on, because all centers are satellites, and all satellites are centers. In other words, satellites follow centers and centers follow satellites.

Each of the following pages deal with harmonic resolutions between two specific keys. There are two three note chords in each of the double barred examples; the first belongs to one key, the second belongs to the resoultion key — in both keys, the notes in the grand arpeggios are employed (no fourth step) —

The resolution key "C" was chosen only for the sake of clarity, but of course any key can be resolved to any other key, for instance; resolving from the key of "F" sharp to the key of "E" flat is no different than resolving form the key of "E' flat to the key of "C", relatively speaking, and on and on it goes.

IMMEDIATE RESOLUTION GENERAL REMARKS

All of the voicings in these examples are merely random choices. There are so many more, space does not permit showing them — and of course the basic idea was designed to have the student search for them, and research for them.

Anyone interested in this type of notational test-tubing, should experiment with all kinds of open and closed voicings. The examples shown employ semi closed to closed voicings, because they present a clearer introductory picture of the principle.

In experimenting, add a fourth note, and a fifth note, even though they may have to be sounded in a delayed way — the important point is to paint your harmonic picture and analyze the result; and always remember that the ear will group notes together when they are sounded fairly close together time-wise.

The added voices in these examples (the x'd notes) are intentionally very basic — there are many many more that are not as basic nor obvious, find them, work with them.

The "grande" arpeggio's for each of the keys are shown for referrence purposes to make it easier and also more exacting in checking the notes in both of the grande arpeggio's, without having to turn pages. When experimenting, any note can readily be checked for correctness — don't trust or rely on "ear" guess work — particularly in the early learning stage.

Later on, when the principle becomes more familiar and firmly embedded, to the point where the ear can decern the subtle voice motion differences, the sky is the limit.

SATELLITE PRINCIPLE

Db GRANDE ARPEGGIO

C GRANDE ARPEGGIO

SATELLITE PRINCIPLE

D GRANDE ARPEGGIO

SATELLITE PRINCIPLE

E♭ GRANDE ARPEGGIO

SATELLITE PRINCIPLE

E GRANDE ARPEGGIO

SATELLITE PRINCIPLE

F GRANDE ARPEGGIO

Satellite principle

F# Grande arpeggio

SATELLITE PRINCIPLE

G GRANDE ARPEGGIO

SATELLITE PRINCIPLE

A♭ GRANDE ARPEGGIO

SATELLITE PRINCIPLE

A GRANDE ARPEGGIO

SATELLITE PRINCIPLE

Bb GRANDE ARPEGGIO

SATELLITE PRINCIPLE

B GRANDE ARPEGGIO

GENERAL REMARKS

Because of having to keep track of, and analyze the motion of the various voices, the student is forced to think in terms of lines and therefore has to get away from the block chord type of thinking.

I don't mean to infer that the "block" chord is not important, but, there is a vast difference between just playing "shapes" because they are there and following lines that of course take on all kinds of shapes, notations, and visuallities. The brain exercise involved in keeping track of two or more lines at one time is of great mental value. The mental, physical, gynmastics required to produce and follow these lines is of great value to any instrumentalist, regardless of the instrument he or she plays.

The first reaction to some of the products of satellite motion usually is a kind of physical and mental rejection because the voicings will form notations and shapes that the fingers are not very familiar with. This period of rejection is normal, but usualy does not last long. The reason for this temporary rejection is because the formations are unusual, and some of them are completely different from the usual block patterns that have for so long a time, been familiar old friends to guitar players. Some of the voicings may not sound good harmonically, and one would not want to harp on them, because, when voices are in motion passing each other, crossing each other, moving contrary to each other, the notes involved are not meant to be played as block chords, — in other words, when voices are in motion doing all the things just mentioned, the movement is not supposed to be frozen or stopped — the frames of a motion picture film very seldom make good still pictures.

Always endeavor to be aware of the notes involved in what you are playing, because this is very necessary when improvizing. Also, notice the type of harmonic structure that is being produced by the satellite motion. Try to be aware of all voice motion, try to be conscious of where they are going and where they have been.

Remember that whether the motion is contrary, parallel, or both, the satellite notes are never more than one half tone away from the centers, but, you must also be concious of the fact that there is whole tone motion in every triplex.

By saying that the satellite notes are never more than a half tone away from the prime notes, or centers, doesn't mean that you can't go directly from the lower satellite to the upper satellite which makes a whole tone interval.

In using the motion of the satellites there is wide and varied harmonic change but not register change, no matter how many notes have been moved you're still in the same register neighborhood.

One of the basic benefits from working with this concept is that when working with two lines the mind must be divided in two, (a duet) when working with three voices the mind has to consentrate on three separate voice motions and so on ——

By starting with two lines one can develop (with work of course) the ability to follow two voices simultaneously, it will not be developed overnight, but it is well worth the time and effort.

Remember, one can always immediately resolve, because of never being more than one half tone away from the center notes of the moment.

CHAPTER 6
THE DISPLACED CONCEPT

THE DISPLACED CONCEPT GENERAL REMARKS

This concept/principle was conceived primarily to help visualize and understand the basic relationship of the various keys to each other, both major and minor.

The principle is helpful in the art of composing/improvising because to be able to go where you want to go musically, say what you want to say, and and then be able to get back logically to the ideas of the main theme is the very essence of improvisation. By the term — "getting back" — I don't mean that one has necessarily got to go back to exactly where they started from. I'm referring to a logical resolution, and/or transition as dictated by the musical moment.

This concept is based on the principle of developing the ability to think in, and be able to visualize two or more keys simultaneously — linking them together mentally, as well as physically in the order of their momentary importance. I'm not inferring that guitarists have not thought in more than one key before, however, the principle of the displaced concept may help to broaden this line of thought.

As we know, all keys are surrounded by secondary, or common keys such as the dominant, subdominant majors and minors — relative majors and minors etc. and these keys must be kept in mind at all times, to be able to create music even of the simplest sort.

Think of these keys as secondary keys that also have their secondary keys, that have their secondary keys and so on down the line in order of "their" momentary importance. The importance of these secondary keys is always changing, depending on the mood or mode the composer is trying to create. This concept covers all of the keys, and relates them to each other — take the key of "C" for instance; the common secondary keys are usually thought to be "G" "F" "DM" "AM" etc. But their are many more; in fact all the keys can be thought of as common to each other — here is an example:

If we start with the key of "C", the dominant key is "G", which has the minor seventh essence of "E" minor, "E" minor has the subdominant major sound of the key of "D" (remember that these are just a few examples) "E" minor is the subdominant minor of "B" — "E" minor is also part of the "A" ninth family — "E" minor also contains the essence of the augmented seventh, with the flatted ninth. Of the key of "A flat. "G" also has the suspended seventh/eleventh essence of the key of "D" etc. (The examples mentioned here are based on the triads as voiced in the basic triad scale). "F" is the subdominant key of "C", which enjoys all of the relationships of "G", but a whole tone down which takes us into "F" sharp/"G" flat major. "D" minor contains both the dominant and subdominant sound, because "D" minor can be "F" major sixth and "G" ninth, because it contains all the basic notes except the third. "D" minor is also the subdominant of the key of "A". "A" minor being the relative minor of "C" contains the "C" major sixth sound, and is also the subdominant minor of "E" — it's also an "A" flat augmented seventh with the lowered ninth, and so on —

All of the minors contain the essence of the thirteenth — example; sound a first inversion "E" minor triad against a "G" seventh, and you have a thirteenth.

All majors enjoy a lowered fifth position with the next lower key. "B" flat major contains the "C" eleventh sound — "B" flat contains the essence of the "G" minor seventh — the "E" flat scale, second-step, to second step, contains an "F" minor essence — "F" minor has a dominant/subdominant essence that relates it directly to "E" flat major — "E" flat major contains the sound of a "C" minor seventh — "E" flat sixth can be "C" minor — "C" minor contains the essence of "A" flat major seventh — "A" flat major contains the minor seventh sound of "F" minor — "F" minor is the relative minor of "A" flat — "A" flat major contains the major seventh plus ninth sound of "D" flat — "D" flat is the subdominant key of "A" flat —

"A" flat is also in a lowered ninth, lowered fifth relationship to the key of "G" — "A" flat is the dominant key of "D" flat, and "D" flat is in the lowered fifth position to the key of "C" — "E" minor can be a "C" major seventh — "E" major is in the minor seventh/eleventh aspect to the key of "B" — "B" is the subdominant of "F" sharp — "F" sharp is the subdominant of "C" sharp — there are many more relationships, as will be discovered. All of the keys enjoy these floating changing relatives.

One must think below the surface of these concepts, with their many facets, to find the vast potential.

Treat the sharp keys the same as the flat keys.

Try to visualize the key relationships in terms of the fingerboard. Try to hear them in your mind's "ear."

Use many different scale variations when working with this concept. Use the entire variation or just a small bit — one must take them apart and refashion them to make new versions and patterns.

The way to learn to think in two or more keys at the same time, is to begin as simply as possible. The introduction to the concept should be limited to two keys. The two keys should be as close together as possible, musically and geographically.

Begin with first inversion traids in the key of "C' —

Start by displacing one step at a time, so that the sound and feel of the displacement can be grasped. There are many ways to do this, but space does not permit showing more than just a few; and the few should be enough to clearly demonstrate the principle.

Start with the first step of the scale; later on, any step can begin. Play step-one and two in their normal positions, they play step-two again, but this time sound it one half tone higher, then play the third-step in it's normal place, and continue on with the scale. What has happened is this: the first time the second-step is played, it is in the key of "C". The second time, it is in the keys of "D" flat/"C" sharp/ enharmonically, but the mind must still think key of "C" firstly, "D" flat/"C" sharp secondly —displace each step one-by-one in this manner. In other words, as each step is displaced, all of the other steps remain in their normal places.
Example:

This time there is just one second step, it is the displaced one

Now displace two adjoining steps at a time, then three, then four, etc.; until the only steps left in "C" are the first and eighth steps. Now the key balance has changed, almost all of the scale is in another key, but the key of "C" is still the principle key.

Become aware of the multitude of combinations available such as; displacing steps three, five, seven, — or two, four, six — two, three, five, seven, etc. The afore mentioned are but just a few of the endless combinations. Now displace these steps a whole tone, then a third interval, then a fourth, then a fifth, etc. Employ all intervals — experiment with them.

Another facet of this concept is this thought line — any step of any scale can become any other step of another scale, at any time —

Use imagination, create more displacements; it's an open field, displace three keys, four keys, etc. Here is a little example of displacing just one step; play the first and second steps of "C", in "C" — now play the second step of the "E" flat scale, now play the second step of the "F" sharp scale, now finish with the eighth step of the "C" scale. These simple little steps make a phrase that resolves; it's very basic but it's honest — think of the many ways it can be elaborated upon, and extended, etc. — but the important point, is that this little cadence, as simple as it is, has involved three keys — by displacing the second-step twice; Example:

Now with a simple bass line

When experimenting with this principle, employ many varied voicings and use closed voicings, open voicings, and voicings in between.

In as many different ways as possible; but while doing this it is very necessary to be conscious of every experimental result — many times an interesting harmonic result from an experiment will, or can, slip by because of a lack of concentration — of course it will be re-discovered later on, maybe alot later on, and this could turn out to be a costly delay.

What usually happens in working with concepts such as these is; one idea suggests another, then that one triggers another idea. It becomes a long endless chain, and that is exactly what is supposed to happen.

DISPLACED CONCEPT – DISPLACING ONE SCALE STEP AT A TIME, THEN TWO, THEN THREE ETC.

DISPLACED CONCEPT

As we know, the three triad inversions can be used just like single notes in many instances to describe a larger chord, either struck together or singly.
Example:

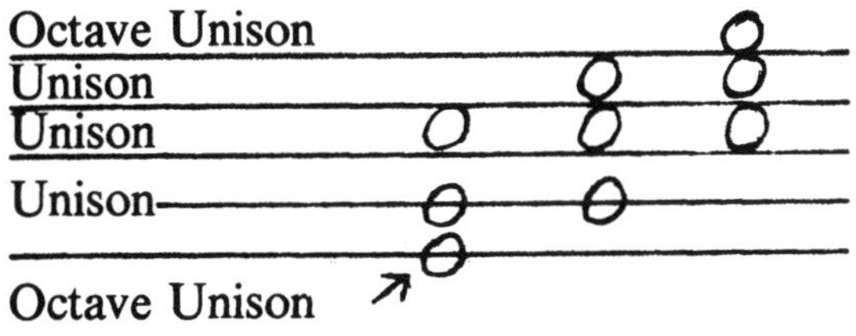

The tonic first inversion naturally represents "C", the tonic second inversion represents "E", the tonic third or root inversion represents the fifth —

The nine notes have great power because of the doubles when sounded together, but harmonically the sum total of the nine voices is just the tonic, third, and fifth —

All three make a very pure "C" chord, but when the notes of the grande arpeggio are employed the results are quite different —
Example:

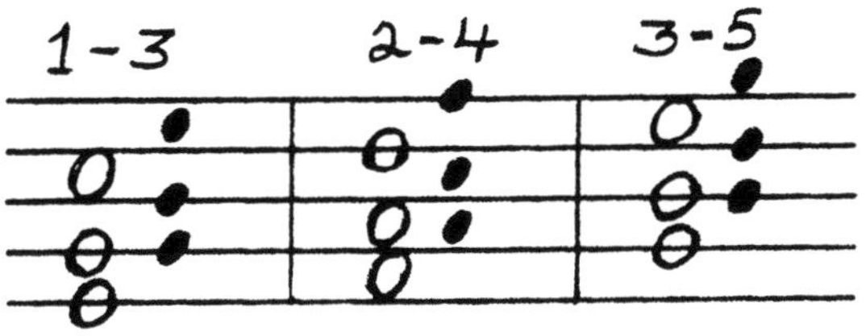

If this were to be orchestrated, just one "G", "A", "B", would be written, unless the power of the unisons were needed.

The use of the word "orchestrate" is quite correct in this instance, because in the playing of the various keyboard instruments, (the guitar is one of them) Orchestration takes place because the harmonic product is a score/orchestration —

It might be appropriate at this time to inform those that do not know, that the guitar is the third most complete instrument we know of — the pipe organ is number one, it is the full orchestra — the piano and all of it's relatives are number two, then comes the guitar, then the harp. The reason that the guitar is third in line, is because it can be played staccato and chromatically rapidly — this is almost impossible on the harp, some players are more apt than others, but it is not the nature of the instrument.

When I was quite young I wrote a rapid chromatic sweep for a harpist in New York, and found out much to my sorrow that it was not playable at that tempo because of having to adjust all of the foot pedals to accomplish it. I'm not putting the harp down, it's a "grande" string instrument that cannot be duplicated by any other instrument.

I merely wish to point out the fact that the little "wooden" string thing we affectionately call a "guitar" is a complete orchestra, (alto, tenor, baritone, bass) that is meant to be played wall-to-wall, as though it were a lap piano —

The complete, the full orchestra, does not have to be accompanied — neither does the organ, piano, guitar, harp, when played with the basic potential in mind.

In the following triad examples steps one, three, five, six, make a "C" major arpeggio using the notes of the "grande" arpeggio — steps two, four, seven, must be omitted because they contain the fourth of the key, and the fourth (F) would give the arpeggio in unsettled, unresolved sound. Of course this situation can change; it depends on the selected triads and voicings.

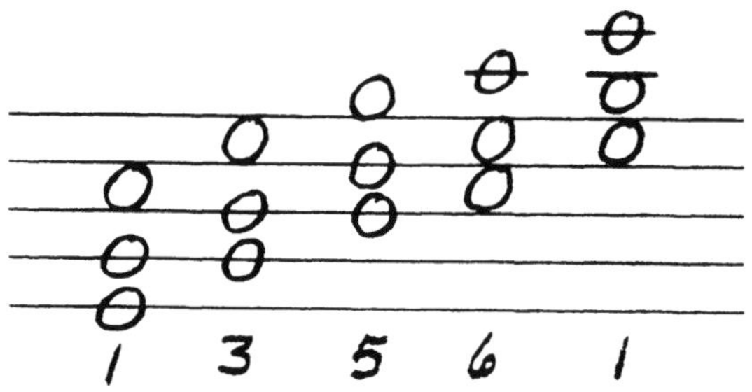

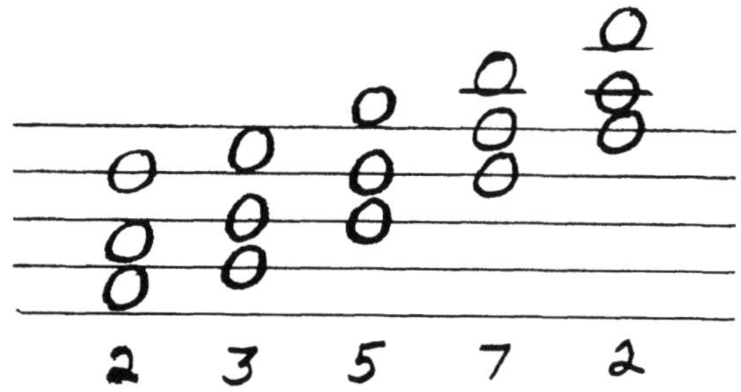

The above examples may appear to be quite childish and very basic, but it must be remembered that every one of these triads can have great depth and many callings,. it all depends on what has taken place harmonically before and after their use. — Step three can be a "C" major seventh, "E" minor, "A" ninth, "G" sixth, "G" thirteenth, "E" flat augmented seventh with the lowered ninth, etc. The harmonic meaning of these triads fully depends on their voicing and use. They can be very trite, or very sophisticated. It all depends on what has been said, and what is going to be said.

Steps two, three, five, seven, contain the notes of the dominant seventh grande arpeggio — in essence, these triads can have, or create many modes and inferences, depending on how they are aligned and how they are thought of.

In all of the different concepts (the chromatic, the stagger, the satellite, the displaced, etc.) notational and key relationships go on, and on, and on, it's endless.

The ideal is to have the mind trained to think in all of these relationships, and then explore as many of the combinations as possible in order to have the principles involved handy mentally and physically, so that they can always be ready and useable.

The notations that follow show a few more basic examples of halt tone motion employing the displaced, stagger, satellite, concepts in progressional form.

In the first three examples the beginning three steps are pure first inversion triads, the fourth step employs the displaced and satellite principle, and could also be the third step with the top note moved a half tone up, and the middle note moved down a half tone (using the satellite notes). Changing it thought-wise in this case to an "E" flat major ninth, although in different harmonic situations it could have other names, such as a "C" eleventh if it were to go into the key of "F" (as it does in example three) — the fourth step can also be thought of as the first step, with the top note staggered one step up the "C" scale, and then displaced a minor third up, thereby placing it on the dominant side of "A" flat, as in examples one and two, to begin the half tone gravitational resolution back to "C".

In the third example, the "C" eleventh leads into "F", then the chromatic lines gravitate back to "C".

Examples six, seven, eight, show displaced mixtures of open and closed voicings.

Bars three and four, of example eight, are shown enharmonically. This was done because the essence of the two keys is different; the first goes into "A" flat, the second goes into "G' sharp, the general mood of the two keys is different.

DISPLACED CONCEPT

The interval gap between the two keys, in the following examples, was chosen only because they are as far apart as two keys can possibly get. The keys of "G" and "D" flat ("C' sharp) were selected at random. As has been mentioned before, any two, three, etc. keys can be employed — any interval between keys can be employed —

Mixtures of the keys can be employed —

Mixtures of the results of the mixtures can be employed, etc. etc. etc. —

When mutations such as these are experimented with, it becomes necessary to work them out on paper in an orderly way, because, when left to memory, there is the element of chance, and results may be errors, and there is nothing worse than a compounded mistake.

DISPLACED CONCEPT

THE LAYOUT FOR TWO KEYS

Db (C#)

G

ANY COMBINATION OF KEYS MAY BE USED

THE TWO KEYS 1 TO 1 IN 1 STAVE

ALTERNATED

THERE ARE MANY BASS/4th VOICE LINES, EXPERIMENT WITH THEM

CHAPTER 7
PROGRESSIVE MOTION

THE PROGRESSIVE MOTION CONCEPT INTRODUCTION

The concept is basically this:

Each voice in a chord is moved diatonically, one-by-one, landing on every note in the "grande arpeggio", for the purpose of forming all of the possible voice combinations the arpeggio contains —

PROGRESSIVE MOTION

Explanation of the "grande arpeggio" notations for the basic modes — All of the notes/intervals in each of the following descriptions can be sounded together as one big chord, or in decreasingly smaller groups or notes. Quite naturally the notes cannot be sounded together on the guitar. They can be struck simultaneously on piano, organ, etc. producing a very rich harmonious sound, but the notes in these arpeggios are meant to be employed selectively. In mentioning the total chord, I'm merely referring to the fact that every note in each "grande" arpeggio is harmonically sympathetic to all the others in that particular "grande arpeggio" —

The guitarist must be notationally selective. The guitarist must be notationally stingy, meager, cunning, almost deceptive yet honest, in order to weave a complete harmonic structure. This can be accomplished by careful thought and practice.

These examples are based on the Key of "C" but apply to all keys:

tonic 3rd 6th
The major intervals are: C - D - E - G - A - B - (No 4th)
2nd 5th 7th

tonic 3rd 6th
The dominant seventh intervals are: G - A - B - D - E - F - (No 4th)
2nd 5th 7th

tonic 3rd 5th
The minor seventh intervals are: D - E - F - G - A - C - (No 6th)
2nd 4th 7th

tonic 3rd 5th
The harmonic minor intervals are: C - D - E♭ - F - G - B - (No 6th)
2nd 4th 7th

The melodic minor intervals are: all of them —

The following notational examples are shown in groups of three notes. (trios) Some of the very close voicings may be out of reach, but are playable when the notes are re-distributed, register-wise, but as written the inforamtion is important, because one must know where the notes have been, and where they can go.

PROGRESSIVE MOTION – MAJOR GRANDE ARPEGGIO = NO FOURTH
15 VOICINGS IN EACH OCTAVE

OCTAVES

PROGRESSIVE MOTION – MINOR SEVENTH GRANDE ARPEGGIO = NO SIXTH

PROGRESSIVE MOTION- DOMINANT SEVENTH GRANDE ARPEGGIO= NO FOURTH

PROGRESSIVE MOTION – HARMONIC MINOR GRANDE ARPEGGIO = NO SIXTH

PROGRESSIVE MOTION—MELODIC MINOR GRANDE ARPEGGIC= COMPLETE SCALE

21 VOICINGS IN EACH OCTAVE

THE PROGRESSIVE MOTION CONCEPT
GENERAL REMARKS
THE "GRANDE ARPEGGIOS"

1. Every note in the major grande arpeggio is compatible with the major chord —
2. Every note in the dominant seventh grande arpeggio is compatible with the seventh chord —
3. Every note in the minor seventh grande arpeggio is compatible with the minor seventh chord —
4. Every note in the harmonic minor grande arpeggio is compatible with the minor chord —
5. Every note in the ascending melodic minor scale is compatible with the minor chord —

The statements above are basically honest, but they are not meant to infer that all of the notes in any grande arpeggio be sounded as one big chord. They should not be sounded that way on any instrument or orchestrated that way, unless a notationally thick, very busy, over arranged sound is desired. In other words, the resulting huge chord would be over seasoned with notational additives such as 2nds/9ths — 6ths — 7ths etc. —

As has been mentioned before, the notes in the grande arpeggios are meant to be used selectively, sparingly, taste and proportion must rule.

CHAPTER 8
DIMINISHED STUDIES

DIMINISHED STUDIES
GENERAL REMARKS

This chapter really should be headlined "diminished and seventh studies", but this was deemed unnecessary because most people that have had some musical schooling know that they are related; but it is hoped that the following material will augment this knowledge, by showing just how very, very closely related they really are.

The minor third intervals —

The diminished chords are like chameleons, they constantly change their colors.

Minor third intervals create many different musical pictures and because of this flexibility the diminished chord is in a category all its own. These intervals swim freely though major and minor harmonic structures providing links in progressions of all kinds.

A diminished triad can be named by any one of the notes in the chord.

Lowering any one of the notes one half tone creates a diminished second that also belongs to the diminished chord a minor third down. This example shows the close relationship:

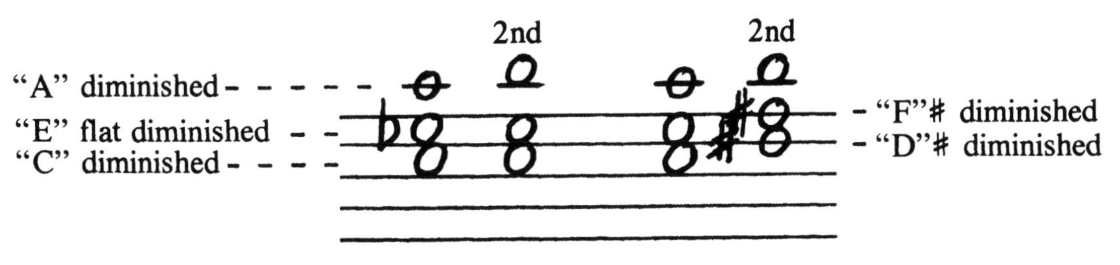

The example shows that raising the voice a whole tone produces a diminished second — it also shows that lowering the top voice of the next higher diminished chord one half tone produces a diminished second but in a closer voicing.

This condition exists with any of the voices in any pure diminished chord.

In other words, the pure major triads; first, second, and third inversion are diminished seconds —

The diminished minor third intervals present notational problems. In order to write/spell consecutive minor thirds so that the interval doesn't look like a second or fourth interval, a mixture of accidentals must be employed, but even then, there will be situations in writing the notations, where the minor third doesn't look like a minor third. Therefore, it is highly advisable to read this material very carefully, particularly the first time.

These studies do not make good "sight reading" material; this applies to all of the studies in these books.

WARNING —
Be prepared to run into enharmonic notational spelling because in places it will happen in adjoining measures. In other words, in some of the studies the beginning of the very next bar will contain the same notes as the last bar but the notational spelling will be written enharmonically.

Always bear in mind that "similar" is not to be mistaken for "identical". Many of the study forms will look "similar", but in analysis will turn out to be quite different. The mental and physical aspects can vary so much, that a broad line seems to separate them. And of course the ideal is for them to become entirely individual, and yet very closely related mentally.

DIMINISHED STUDIES

QUARTER NOTE STEMS OMITTED

DIMINISHED STUDIES

DIMINISHED STUDIES - ARTICULATED SIXTHS

MOVE THESE EXAMPLES CHROMATICALLY UP AND DOWN THE FINGERBOARD

DON'T LET THREE VOICES SOUND AT THE SAME TIME, IT'S A DUET OF VOICES

REPEAT MANY TIMES TO SET THE PHYSICAL PICTURE, USE THE ABOVE FINGERING

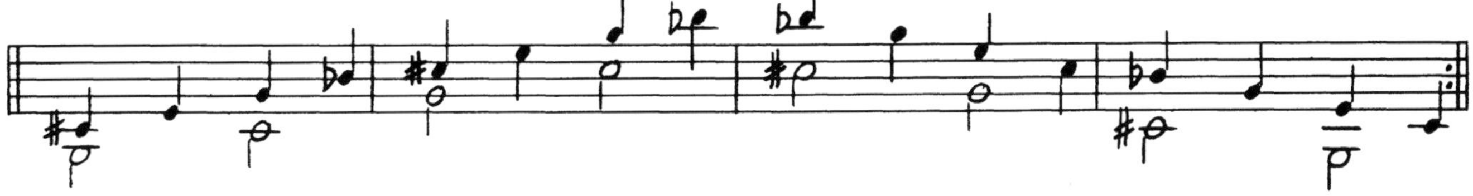

MOVE THIS UP AND DOWN AS FAR AS POSSIBLE, SLOWLY AT FIRST

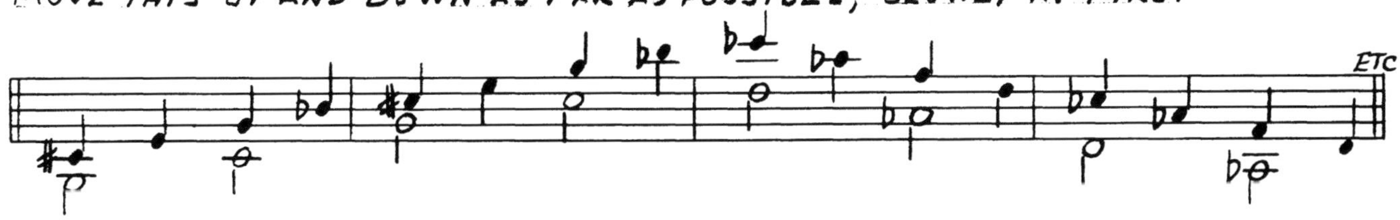

DIMINISHED STUDIES – THE DIMINISHED ARPEGGIO IN 6THS AND 10THS

DIMINISHED STUDIES

DIMINISHED STUDIES

DIMINISHED STUDIES

COMBINE THE VARIOUS FORMS- BLEND THEM

DIMINISHED STUDIES

DIMINISHED STUDIES

ON C DIM

ABOVE: THE MAJOR TRIAD IS ALSO A DIMINISHED 2ND OR 9TH - THIS APPLIES TO THE 2ND AND ROOT INVERSIONS ALSO

ON B DIM

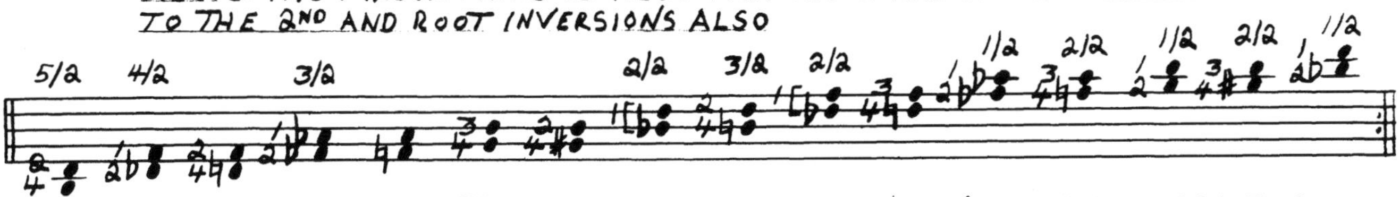

THE TOP VOICE DESCRIBES THE ARPEGGIO - THE LOWER VOICE DESCRIBES THE DIMINISHED SCALE = WHOLE TONE, HALF TONE, WHOLE TONE, HALF TONE, ETC

IN THIS EXAMPLE EVERY OTHER CHORD IS A RELATED DIMINISHED CHORD, THEY ARE "LINKS" THAT BECOME DOMINANT 7TH CHORDS WITH THE LOWERED 9TH

GENERAL REMARKS

All seventh chords belong to the family of diminished chords, and all diminished chords belong to the family of seventh chords —

Example: (All 4 Voices =)

"B" Dim "G" 7th "B"♭7th

"B" Dim "F" Dim

All four voices also make a "B flat seventh with a lowered ninth in the upper voice —

The followng examples explain the premise further;

As diminished chords

As diminished chords

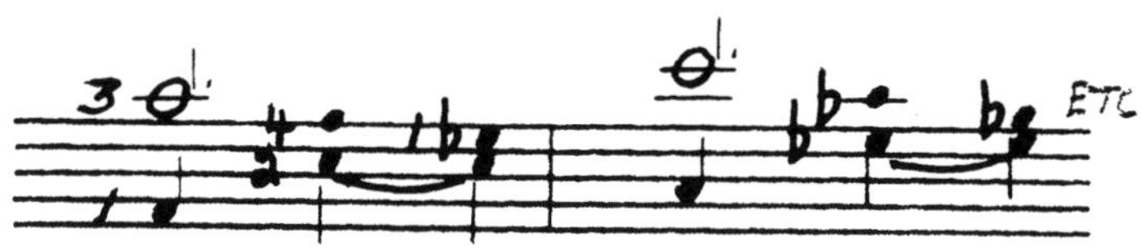

As seventh chords

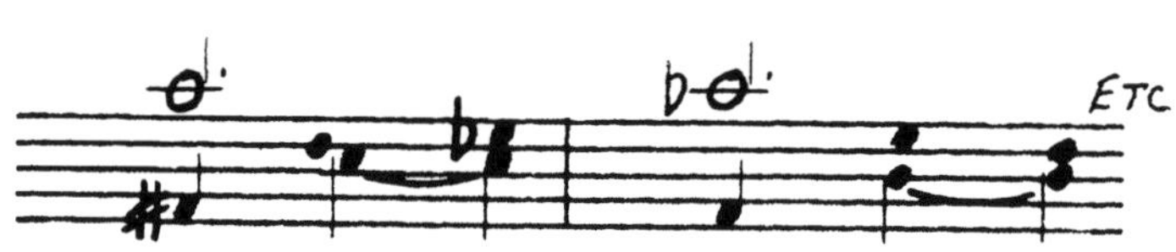

Continue on through the cycle of 5ths

The close relationship between diminished chords and seventh chords —

The following examples basically show how the diminished voicings relate to seventh chords — they demonstrate that the two notations are always interwoven, in other words, they occupy the same space musically.

All three = "A" Dim.

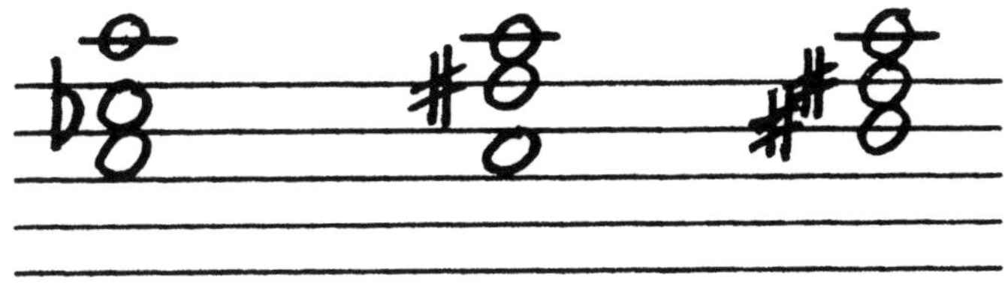

Now with a fourth voice

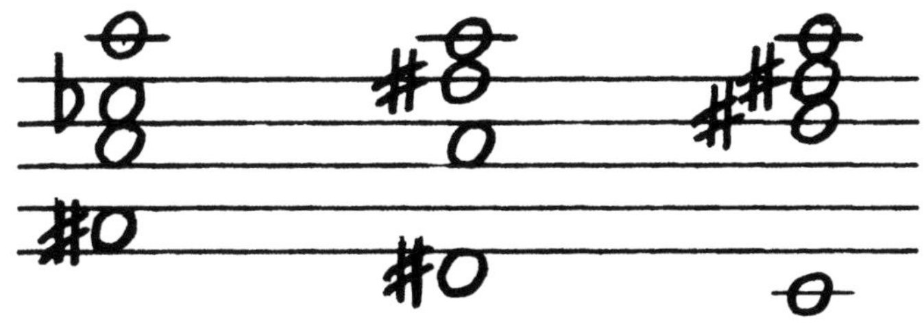

Now as seventh chords

Now, in 3 voices the 7th and the diminished together

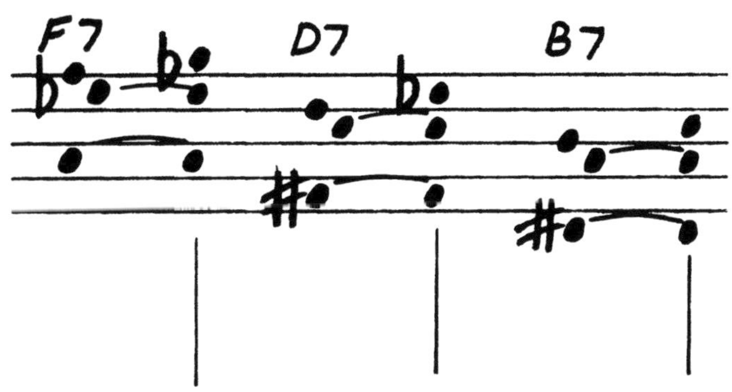

G♭ Dim and B7 | E♭ Dim and A♭7 | C Dim and F7

Quite naturally all of the seventh chords follow the minor third intervals of the diminished arpeggio —

Examples of two seventh chords containing each other:

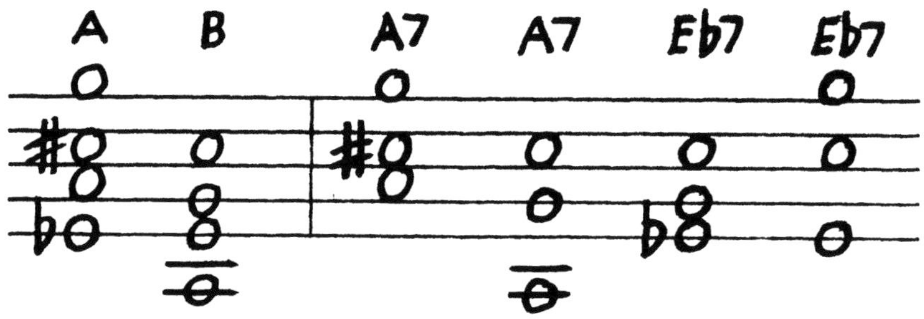

Above: These two identical voicings in two locations contain the last four seventh chords — in other words, voicings A, and B, contain each other in the lowered fifth essence.

The examples below are very closely related to the above example and can be continued through the cycle of fifths —

DIMINISHED STUDIES

DIMINISHED STUDIES - REPEAT THESE EXAMPLES EVERY 3 FRETS

DIMINISHED NOTATIONS EMPLOYING STAGGERED NOTES BASED ON "A" DIMINISHED

DIMINISHED AND SEVENTH EXAMPLES

PROGRESSIONS IN SEVENTHS AND DIMINISHED CHORDS

SEVENTHS THRU THE CYCLE OF 5THS FALLING INTO PLACE FROM A HALF TONE ABOVE

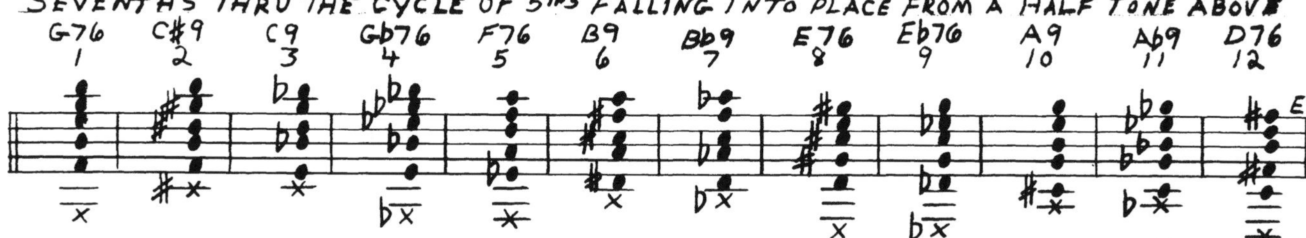

THE LOW "D" IS SHOWN FOR CONTINUIT

SAME BASS LINE, BUT THE ABOVE CHORDS ARE IN REVERSE ORDER

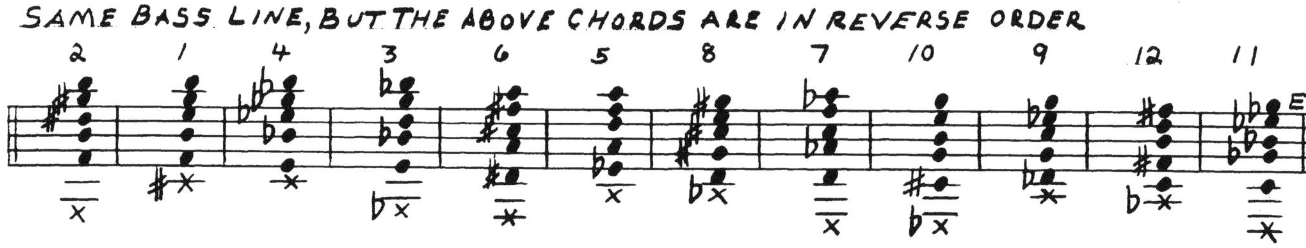

GENERAL REMARKS

As has been undoubtedly noticed, the dividing line between the diminished mode and the seventh mode is almost invisable — these two modes are harmonic, tonal chameleons — musically, it all depends on how they are used and when they are used.

MISCELLANEOUS REMINISCENCE
CHAPTER 9
ARTICULATED 6ths TO 11ths
PROGRESSIONS
CONTRARY MOTION

GENERAL REMARKS
THE ELOQUENCE OF ANDRÉS SEGOVIA

"One must make love to the instrument"

In an exceptance speech for an honorary degree, one of his remarks was; "I have traveled the world so many times I can feel the curvature of the earth beneath my feet" —

GENERAL REMARKS

The use of the alphabet, words, numbers, etc. does not require muscle, it does not require physical dexterity — it requires mental dexterity.

Learning the different concepts requires mental dexterity, applying the notations in the studies and examples requires a knowledge of the physical mechanisms — physical dexterity —

Blending mental and physical mechanisms is the very essence of the chemistry necessary to be able to play well.

The chemistry begins with an idea, (mental) it is coupled to a picture, a mental picture of the physical mechanisms required to produce the idea — that mental picture has the last word. It is either right or wrong —

All experiments are worthless, when the results are forgotten —

When a study is more than one stave long, the key signature, when used, will appear in the first bar only and therefore must be remembered for the remainder of the study —

ARTICULATED 6THS – 9THS TO 10THS

MAJOR

TIME VARIATION SUSTAIN WHOLE NOTE FULL VALUE

GENERAL REMARKS

Always bear in mind that all accidentals are canceled by bar lines unless tied over to the following bar—

ARTICULATED 6THS – 9THS TO 10THS

MELODIC MINOR

HARMONIC MINOR

CONTRARY MOTION 9TH TO 11TH MAJOR

CONTRARY MOTION 9TH TO 11TH MELODIC MINOR

- CONTRARY MOTION - 9TH TO 11TH HARMONIC MINOR

CONTRARY MOTION

MAJOR

ROOT 1ST 2ND

MELODIC MINOR

HARMONIC MINOR

CONTRARY MOTION

CONTRARY MOTION – DEVELOP THIS CONCEPT OF INVERSION

GENERAL REMARKS
PROGRESSION

Webster's Dictionary describes the meaning of the term "progression" in these words; "The movement of musical parts in harmony" —

Also; "A succession of musical tones"

Moving one or two notes just one half tone almost always changes the musical meaning and direction of a progression quite a bit —

Every step in a progression, long or short, is a musical switch track so to speak, that can send the voices in many different directions. Experimenting with, and taking advantage of all the opportunities and possibilities these switch tracks provide is, I believe, the best teacher.

I'm not a musicologist as such, but, as far as I know there are no set formulas or rules for "progression", just as there are no set formulas or rules for taste.

Voices can go any direction at any time, the harmony can ascend, descend, move sideways, zig-zag, etc. Most of the time progressions are a mixture of all the afore mentioned and the musically artistic result depends on the composers sense of balance, proportion, and taste.

Progressions come in all sizes, they can be smooth and flowing, while others can be quite disjointed and still sound pleasing to the ear. The only real test for music is time — does it wear well, does a person want to hear it again and again, or is once enough.

I don't mean to infer that progressions are "things" set apart from the music itself. "Progression" is the very heart of music — and that is why short, and semi-long progressions must be worked with and studied carefully in order to be able to understand the complete freedom voices can enjoy.

Progression is a wonderfully exciting independant form that does not have to belong to any one key or mode.

I like to think of the term "progression" as a huge constantly flowing river of ever changing musical tones that can be tapped into from all angles and attitudes, upstream, downstream, midstream, bottom, top, etc.

When an inquisitive artistic mind taps into this river of flowing tones, the results are usually very interesting, and many times, exciting. Some progressions can be slyly deceptive as the following little example shows;

It is deceptive because steps two and four have been positioned purposely to sound like, and take the place of "D" and "G" diminished chords, when in fact they are seventh chords — the second step is an "A" flat 13th — the fourth step is an "E" flat 9th — in other words, they are the dominant sevenths of "D" flat and "A" flat — and both are switch tracks into many other keys.

Quite often dominant sevenths can substitute for sub dominant minors — if the second step of this example was thought of as a sub dominant minor, it would be taking the place of an "E" flat minor and therefore would be in the sub dominant minor position to the key of "B" flat.

The fourth step would be in the sub dominant position of "F" etc., etc.

The whole idea is to create a progressional premise, a basic harmonic structure to work with, no matter how disjointed it may be. Maybe it should be disjointed, maybe not, if it is the latter, try to rejoin the voices, rework them so as to conform with your original mental picture of the idea — the important thing is to stay with it, work it out. When "things" don't go very well, it's easy to procrastinate and go to something else. This can very easily turn into a bad habit.

It is very important to stay with each idea while the ideas are flowing and try to remember all of the experimental variations. This is very important and necessary for future reference.

Play these progressions very slowly at first, remember, there is no need to hurry —

PROGRESSION

PROGRESSION
CON

PROGRESSION

PROGRESSION
MISCELLANEOUS REMINISCENCE

The following short examples have not been shown before in these books. A few of them may seem to be similar in places, but as has been mentioned before, similar is not identical. Each one contains slight variations of the original.

In this group of examples I have purposely repeated the opening progressional premise, then little subtle changes, slight adjustments, take place. Voice leading changes, not much, but enough to affect the direction of the progression.

Small changes in voice motion can change the intent and resolution because one slight change suggests another, and another, and another, etc. This process gradually changes the sound color and character of the progression — in other words, it is a good way to experiment with any and all harmonic ideas.

I have purposely avoided describing (symbolizing) the various steps in these progressional examples because it all depends on what you hear them to be.

When lines are in motion, independent of each other, and are flowing freely they should not be frozen into chords as such, because then they are taken out of context, progression, is motion.

Fingerings are shown in these progressional studies only when deemed necessary to clarify specific combinations of mechanisms —

Try not to hurry these, play them slowly and accurately because they are not velocity studies.

Notice subtle differences in the combinations of mechanisms, etc.

PROGRESSION

PROGRESSION

7

8

9

10

PROGRESSION

11 

12 

13 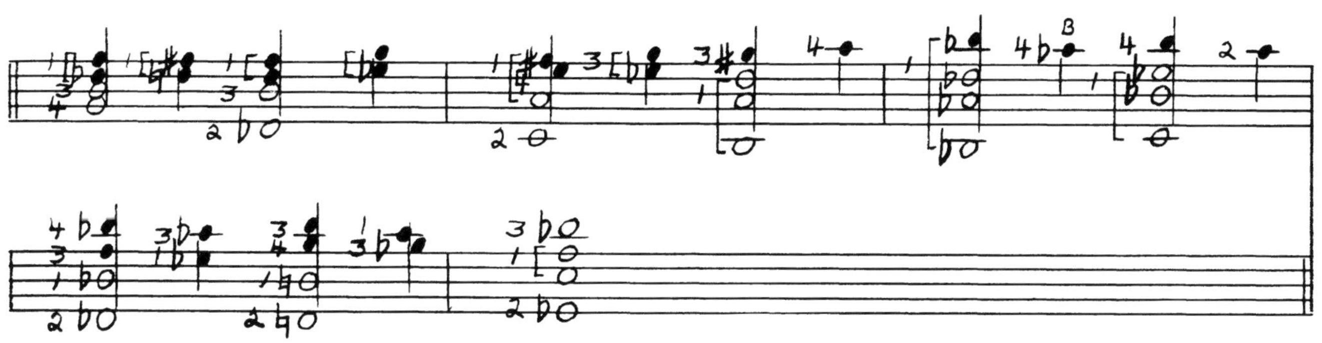

PROGRESSION

14

A VARIATION OF 14

15

16

GENERAL REMARKS
PROGRESSION

The following short studies are examples that are meant to be extended, they are merely suggestions, mix the basic ideas they present and endeavor to add new ideas to them —

GENERAL REMARKS
MISCELLANEOUS REMINISCENCE
"THE CONTINUOUS LOOP"

The first four bars show the basic fingering necessary to continue the loop, which of course is a continuous circle of fifths.

All of the steps encompass three strings, but just two voices should sound simultaneously; three should not sound together unless the closeness of the second interval is desired.

Change registers any place, ascend as far as possible, descend as far as possible, stay in one position and cross all four sets of strings, etc. The continuous loop is found on the lower half of the first page of "short examples" —

PROGRESSION— SHORT EXAMPLES

CONTINUOUS LOOP-CIRCLE 5

KEEP REPEATING

PROGRESSION
CONTINUOUS LOOP PRACTICE

Many of the work studies in these books are based on the circle/cycle of fifths, those so based, can become continuous loops —

PROGRESSION

Again, do not carry over accidentals to the next bar unless the notes are tied — this is very important.

PROGRESSION

PROGRESSION

PROGRESSION

PROGRESSION